Mr. Nightmare

Cover design by Matt Seff Barnes
All rights reserved. Copyright © 2022 Joe Scipione
All rights reserved.
Wicked House Publishing

Dedication

For Mandy, Tom and Isabella. I couldn't do this without you.

Acknowledgements

Sometimes stories come in bits and pieces. This one didn't. I had the idea for the story while working out and listening to music. An hour later I knew all the major plot points and I was ready to write.

Writing a book is a solitary activity but it takes a lot of people working together to publish one. A million thanks to everyone who helped make this book possible. My publisher Patrick Reuman has been helpful and supportive through the entire process. Thanks to Matt Barnes for creating an incredible cover that looks remarkably similar to the idea I had in my head. Kenneth W. Cain for finding all of the mistakes I made along the way and making the story better. Dave LaSota for reading an early version of this and always having great advice and seeing things I don't. Thanks also to David LaForest, Michelle Welsh and Jenn Moreale for their help putting the first few chapters together and getting Mr. Nightmare off to a strong start. Thanks to Douglas Ford for his kind words and taking the time to read this ahead of publication. Mandy, Tom and Isabella for putting up with me and letting me get into the writing zone one or two times a day. I couldn't have done this without them. Most of all thanks to you, the reader, for picking up this book and giving my weird, scary story a shot. I hope you like it.

Joe Scipione - October 2022

MR. NIGHTMARE

A Novel

Joe Scipione

Chapter 1

I can't tell you the exact moment the Nightmare Club changed, but when things went south, it got bad fast. I remember the day we started the club like it was yesterday, even though the group was formed in the summer of 1985. Actually, it was John Workman who first had the idea, but you can't start a club by yourself, so he needed us.

The first meeting of our little group was just me, Chuck, and John. I guess you could say we were the founders, but like I said, it was all John's idea. We just went along with it. Eventually, Marcus Truant and Merrie O'Day joined us. That was really when it felt like an actual club for the first time.

Chuck, John, and I were inseparable from the time we were in third grade. I was just in second grade back then. Because of that, when it was just the three of us, it always felt like more of the same. When we added more people, it felt different. More so when

Marcus and Merrie joined us. But I'm getting a little ahead of myself.

A lot of guys wouldn't just hang out with their younger sister, but Chuck and I were so close in age that we did everything together. He always felt more like a friend to me than an older brother, anyway.

The day John came up with the idea for the Nightmare Club, it was summer vacation between seventh and eighth grade for me. The summer before the boys would go into high school. Usually, after the first few weeks, we ran out of things to do. Eventually, we ended up sitting down at The Field in one of the dugouts, just thinking of things we could do to entertain ourselves.

"I got an idea," John said, his mouth full of pink bubblegum. He had his glove on his left hand and was throwing the baseball against the inside wall of the dugout. He repeatedly caught it before it bounced past him. "Let's sneak out tonight and tell scary stories or something in the woods. It'll be fun."

"Yeah," Chuck agreed right away.

Chuck was the perfect kid. He got good grades and was nice to everyone, but he always went along with what John suggested, even if it was something he wouldn't normally do. Sneaking out, for example. If I ever said we should sneak out of the house after Mom and Dad were asleep, Chuck would talk about how much trouble we'd get in if we got caught. No way Chuck would go along with what I said. But I didn't take it personally. Chuck looked up to John. They were best friends.

I think Chuck was a little jealous of John. He wished he could be so carefree. To let loose and not care what others thought of him. Chuck worried too much. So, when John had an idea, he usually went for it.

"What about you Anna-banana? You in?" John popped a big bubble and whipped the baseball at the cement wall again.

In a sense, I had more in common with John than I did with my own brother, because John probably knew what I was going to say before he even asked. I didn't mind stretching the rules a little if it meant I'd have a few hours of fun and adventure.

"Yup," I said. "I'm in."

Chuck gave me a look. It wasn't disappointment exactly, more like a look of judgment. Don't really know how he could judge me after he just agreed to the same thing, but I was used to that too. It never changed things between us. He was still my brother and my best friend, and he'd look out for me. In his head, it was all part of his job.

He smiled after I caught his glance. I grinned back.

"Great," John said. "I'll meet you guys at the corner around one tonight. My parents are always up late, so I need to make sure they're asleep first."

We nodded.

'The corner' was the intersection of Marshall Circle—the cul-de-sac we lived on—and George Lane, which was the cross street. Both were relatively slow when it came to traffic but had streetlights and sidewalks running down both sides so, even though it was late, we wouldn't be totally in the dark.

It wasn't difficult for us to get out of the house. Chuck's room was right next to mine, and since we lived in a single-story ranch, sneaking out meant popping open a window and squeezing through. We'd made a plan for Chuck to get out first. When he tapped on my window, I'd join him and we'd be on our way.

Around ten that night I said goodnight to Mom, Dad, and Chuck and went to bed. I knew Chuck wouldn't be far behind me. I kept my regular clothes on instead of changing into sweats for bed, but slipped under my covers and closed my eyes. Any other night, if I'd laid in bed with my eyes closed, I would have eventually dozed off. But I was too excited that night.

I lay on my side, my ear throbbing as blood rushed through. I was ready to hop out of bed at a moment's notice. It didn't even matter to me why we were sneaking out, as it was more about the act of getting out of the house when we weren't supposed to than the purpose for leaving. I would have snuck out for anything. Or no reason at all.

It felt like forever, but eventually I heard the light tap of Chuck's fingertip against my window. My eyes snapped open, and I pulled my legs out from under my covers and grabbed my shoes. I didn't put them on because we had hardwood floors in our bedrooms—one wrong step and my parents were sure to hear. That was what I assumed; everything sounds louder late at night when the house is quiet.

I slid open my window as slowly and noiselessly as it allowed. It always creaked a little bit and I knew there was nothing I could do about it, but I wanted to avoid slamming it open. That had happened once before and it shook the house. If that happened tonight, our little adventure—and the Nightmare Club—would have ended before it even started.

I got the window up, and Chuck helped me through and onto the cool grass. I slipped one shoe on, then the other, and we were off. We didn't say a word to each other until we were a good twenty or thirty steps down the road.

"You think they heard us?" Chuck asked.

I could tell he was nervous. He would be until we met up with John.

"I don't think so. If they did, we'll be in some shit, though." I smirked, knowing it was killing him a little inside. He'd calm down soon and enjoy the adventure, but I could tease him until then. That's what little sisters were for.

It wasn't long before we were at the corner. The only sound were the crickets chirping and the occasional gust of wind. John wasn't there, but we knew we'd left a few minutes early and planned to wait for him.

"I'm sure they didn't hear us. They wouldn't just let us sneak out if they heard us. They would have chased after us. At least Dad would have. Mom—who knows what she would have done? Probably would have chased us down the street with a wooden spoon." Chuck laughed.

I could tell he was relaxing. I could practically hear it in his voice as he talked.

"Yeah, I think we should be okay. What do you think John has in mind? Sometimes he comes up with the craziest ideas."

"I know. Who knows what he's got up his sleeve? He's like the activities director for our group— always has some game for us to play. Never a dull moment." Chuck laughed, and I joined him.

The crunch of sneakers on gravel behind us broke the laugher and made us both turn at the same time. My heart fluttered for a moment, but I knew John was coming any second. Then I saw his smiling face, lit up from underneath by a flashlight.

"It's too late for you kiddies to be out here by yourself," he said in a low, scratchy voice.

"What'd you bring that for?' Chuck asked, ignoring John's joke and motioning to the flashlight.

"Oh, I got three of them. One for each of us, for the woods. Don't turn 'em on yet." John returned to his normal voice and handed a flashlight to Chuck, then reached in his pocket and pulled out a smaller one and handed it to me. "For you, Anna-banana."

I took the flashlight.

He pulled out another small one from his other pocket and looked at us then nodded his head to the right. "Come on. We're off."

We walked for about half an hour. There was no real way to tell. John led us through our neighborhood, then down Red Bird Drive, which was a dead end. At the end of the street, there was a single street light illuminating the road and the edge of the woods beyond. It was obviously there to let people driving know there was no more road.

Stories had long circulated among kids in our neighborhood about someone driving down the road before any of us lived in the neighborhood. Legend had it, some guy had been driving thirty miles an hour down Red Bird, not realizing it was a dead end, and ended up crashing into a tree somewhere in the woods. Supposedly that tree still bore the scars from the front of his car, but I'd never seen it. Of course, it might have just all been bullshit anyway; some legends are nothing but that.

When we reached the end of the street, John stepped off the pavement and made for the woods. "Come on." He pushed a branch out of his way and slipped between a couple of trees. "I got a spot that's perfect for us. It's just up here a way. Then we can sit and start a fire or whatever you guys want. Just trust me, okay?"

We did trust him. We'd all been friends for pretty much as long as we could remember, and I was excited to see where this late-night adventure ended. As I suspected, once Chuck got with John, he was just as eager as I was.

John disappeared into the darkness of the woods and flicked on his flashlight. Chuck did the same. Pulling up the rear, I smiled, flicked my light on, and followed them into the night.

John was right, it didn't take long for us to the reach the little area he knew about. He didn't tell us how he knew about the place, but it wasn't out of the realm of possibility that John was out walking in the woods by himself and stumbled across the spot. There were a few logs laying across the ground that looked as though they'd been pushed into a somewhat circular shape. In the middle sat a steel drum with branches, twigs, and some leaves inside.

"See? What did I tell ya?" John held his arms out to either side showing off the place as if it were a million-dollar living room inside a huge mansion. I couldn't see his face, but I could tell he was smiling.

"Yeah, Johnny. This is pretty sweet." Chuck roamed around the outside edge of the circle of logs.

"Did you put this together or just find it out here?" He shined the flashlight into the woods, the beam reflecting off some of the close trees and bushes, but disappearing into the darkness in other spots.

John either didn't hear the question or chose to ignore it because he never answered. He stood by the barrel, flashlight in his mouth, shining it down at something in his hands.

I went over to join him. "Whatcha doin'?" I shined my light on his hands.

"Oh, check it out, Anna-B." His fingers flicked together and a flame burst out. It was a book of matches. John tossed the burning matches into the barrel.

It wasn't long before the wood inside was burning and we didn't need the flashlights anymore. The flames warmed the air around us. Though it wasn't cold out, the heated air felt good on my skin. After talking about nothing in particular around the burning barrel, the three of us sat down on the logs. When there was a silence that lasted longer than usual, Chuck spoke up.

"So, what did you want to do out here, John? Just hang out and light a fire? I mean, it's cool and all, but you're the activities director; you've always got something planned for us," Chuck said.

We all laughed.

"No, no. I did have an idea, but you're right; it's cool just hanging out here like this. Everyone is asleep and we're out just enjoying the night, you know? Like we should be."

Chuck nodded.

"It's fun, and I don't need to do whatever you had in mind," I said. "But I'm curious."

"Yeah," Chuck agreed.

"For real??" Even in the dull orange-red glow of the fire and the strange moving shadows it cast, I could see John smile when we both wanted to hear his master plan for the evening.

"Of course," I said.

"Okay, let's hear it."

"Okay, so I had this idea… We'd need more people to do it properly but, I figured—you know— you guys are my best friends, so we should like give it a test run. And if you like the idea and it's fun, then we get a few more kids to come with us next time."

John stood up and paced. Then he stopped near the barrel, almost to the point of leaning on it. The fire lit his face from below, the same way he'd done with the flashlight earlier.

"Okay, then. Enough mystery." Chuck threw his hands up. "What is it?"

"Well, so, I was trying to come up with a name for it, and I just wasn't sure if it was good or not." John was talking fast and in circles, like he did when he was excited. "But maybe after you guys hear the idea you could help me think of what to call it. Because I think it should have a really good name, you know? One that shows what it's really all about. But, anyway... I had one, so maybe you could see what you think—"

"John," I interrupted.

"Sure, you're right. Sorry. Thanks, Anna-banana." John took a deep breath to slow himself down, then continued. "I was thinking we get together once a week or so, come out here and tell, like, scary stories and stuff. But we only do one story a night. Then we go home, go to bed, and see if the story gives us nightmares. We would keep score. If I tell a story and you guys both have nightmares that night, I get two points. The next week Chuck goes. If only Anna has a nightmare, then Chuck gets one point. Only one person goes at a time. That way we know who caused the nightmares and it's easy to keep score. Then we just have a scoreboard and maybe a season with a trophy or something. I don't know. But I thought we should call it the Nightmare Club."

I liked the idea before the entire thing had been explained. I didn't need any more details. I was sold. John, Chuck, and I were all very competitive and we played sports. But these boys were a year older than me and it was hard for me to keep up with them when we played anything physical. I could hold my own— especially in basketball—but this would be an even playing field and give us another way to compete. John was right, though; we needed a few more people.

"So, the nightmare part is going to have to be based on the honor system then," Chuck said.

"Yep. I trust you guys," John said. "But we need probably two more people that we can trust to tell the truth. Any ideas?"

Chuck stood up. I did too. We were all excited.

This had happened before, when we figured out a way to play one-on-one-on-one basketball and when we'd invented a new game that could be played with three people with the creative name of *kick 'n catch*. We were used to talking ideas out together, and this had the potential to be one of the great ones. At least it seemed that way to us at the time.

"What about Marcus Truant? He lives around the corner and was on the football team last year. He's pretty cool and a nice kid. I'm sure he'd be trustworthy. I bet he'd be with us on this." Chuck said.

"Would he sneak out at night, though?' I asked.

"Not sure. I'll ask him."

"Anyone else? Any other girls, Anna?" John looked to me. He held his hands out to the fire, letting the warmth lick at his palms, then flipped them over to warm the backs.

"Only other girl in the neighborhood around our age is Merrie O'Day. I don't know her that well, and she's a year younger than me, but I can ask her."

"All right," John said. "That might work. Now, who wants to tell the first story?"

<u>Chapter 2</u>

I never considered that night to be the first meeting of the Nightmare Club because all five of us weren't there, but it was definitely the birth of the club. John told a scary story, but there was nothing remarkable about it. We were young enough and hadn't had much storytelling practice and it showed. Like I said, I'll never forget the day the Nightmare Club changed. Before that could happen though, we needed a few more members. After that first night by the fire and the circle of logs, we left with one job: convince Marcus and Merrie to join us. The boys would work on Marcus, because they both kind of knew him. That left me with the task of convincing Merrie to come along. No one had any nightmares that night, but we weren't keeping score yet, anyway.

"Chuck, I don't even really know her," I said the next morning over a breakfast of cereal and orange juice. Dad was already gone for the day—golfing, I think—by the time we woke up. Mom was in and out of the kitchen doing housework, so it was fairly safe to talk about the Nightmare Club—at least in vague terms.

"I know." Chuck slurped a mouthful of milk and Cookie Crisp, then continued while chewing. "But what are we going to do, send John to invite her? If she's going to agree to come with us, it's going to be because *you* invite her."

He was right, but it didn't make me feel any more comfortable about asking her.

"How should I do it? Just go over to her house and knock on her door?"

He shook his head, swallowed, then answered. "No. She's always outside watching her little sister and playing hula-hoop or jumping rope with her lately— whenever we walk by, at least. Just try to time it up. If she's out, go up and talk to her about other stuff. Ask who she wants for teachers next year or something, then invite her along. You're a friendly person, once you start talking to her, you'll be fine. Hopefully she says yes." He smiled and raised his eyebrows. "I can't wait to beat all your asses. John said he's going to try to find something to use as a trophy. I'm already making space on my bookshelf for it."

"All right," I said, and kicked him under the table. Just then Mom walked in. "That makes sense."

"You two have a busy day planned? You slept late this morning." Mom dropped a basket of laundry on the floor. "Anna, this is yours. Chuck, go grab yours in the basement."

"Same as every day, Mom. We're meeting John at The Field then we'll figure it out once we get there." Chuck took the last scoop of cereal, slurped it, then stood up, dropped his bowl in the kitchen sink, and made for the basement door.

"As long as all your chores are done before you leave. Anna: clothes and trash. Chuck: clothes and dishes."

"We know, Mom," Chuck said, in his usual annoyed tone that always came out when Mom mentioned chores.

"No problem, Mom." I stood and smiled, put my bowl in the sink next to Chuck's, and grabbed the laundry basket.

"Thank you!" Mom said as we both went our separate ways to tend to our chores.

Once done, Chuck and I met on the porch out front, which was where most of our summer days began. It was cool for a Midwestern summer, but we always had a few days that weren't hot mixed in here and there. For the most part, summers in Illinois were hot and dry, except for the occasional thunderstorms and the tornado warnings that often came with them. We'd grown accustomed to them over the years—to the point where the tornado sirens didn't always spark a pang of worry in our stomachs. Sometimes, when the sky was so dark that it looked green and the wind seemed to come out of nowhere, we worried. But most of the time, dark skies and whipping winds just meant it was time to head home.

That day it was too cool to worry about storms, but still hot enough that all we needed was a pair of shorts and a t-shirt, the official uniform of summer.

Chuck leaped over the rail of the porch instead of just walking down the steps. "Want to go find John?"

I sighed. "No. I'm going to walk by Merrie's house to see if I can catch her outside. I want to get this over with."

"Don't be nervous. You're a natural at talking to people, and she's waved at us a bunch of times. She probably wants you to stop and talk to her, anyway."

"Yeah, yeah." I rolled my eyes.

But Chuck was right. He was the smartest of all of us, and not just book smart. Aside from being a little nervous about breaking the rules most of the time, Chuck was the one with the brain. We all knew it. He was good at sports, but half of the reason was the fact that he could out-think whomever he was playing against. Even when John came up with some weird rules for a new game to play, Chuck would figure out the best way to exploit the rules so he could win. And he was a good enough athlete to win at whatever game we happened to be playing.

"Okay, well, just think about what I said. I'll get John and we'll meet you down at The Field."

"All right. And yes, I'll do it your way," I said before we left in opposite directions.

The funny part of the whole thing was that it all went down exactly as Chuck predicted. I bumped into Merrie while she was jumping rope, and we got to talking. She made a joke, and I laughed. I said something funny, and she laughed. It was actually pretty easy, because the more I got to know Merrie, the more I realized we had a lot in common. After about ten minutes, I realized she would probably say yes, so I explained the Nightmare Club to her, and she was genuinely excited by the idea. It couldn't have gone better. I invited her along and, after she checked with her mom, we left to meet John and Chuck at The Field.

The next few days, the four of us played at The Field together. Toward the end of the week, there were even a few appearances from Marcus. He'd also agreed to join the Nightmare Club. We had a few discussions about the club and who would be the first person to tell their story, but most of the time we just did regular kid stuff. Over the course of the week, it felt like our group of three had become a group of five. As Saturday night drew closer, we all got more and more excited about the first official meeting of the Nightmare Club.

Finally, it was Saturday, Chuck and I had to go with Mom to visit our grandparents a few towns away. We made the trip a few times a month if we didn't see

them for other reasons during the week. I didn't mind
going and always had a good time at their house, even
though Chuck and I just ended up watching football or
baseball on the couch with Grandpa. Grandma always
had a tin of mints that were small and chalky. They
disintegrated in your mouth after only a few seconds.
Nothing about them tasted all that great, but I still ate
them. Those mints will always remind me of Saturdays
spent at Grandma's house. We ate dinner; Grandma
had made meatloaf.

After dinner, we returned home. Dad was
already asleep in front of the TV with a can of beer in
his hand. Mom shook her head when we walked into
the living room. Chuck and I sat and stared at the TV,
but I was watching the clock out of the corner of my
eye. Every minute felt like an hour. Time passed
agonizingly slow as we sat there waiting for the night
to be upon us.

At last, it was late enough for me to say I was
tired and so I headed to bed. I even gave a fake yawn.
This caused Mom to yawn for real. I smiled to myself,
went to bed, and a few minutes later heard the old floor
squeak outside my room, meaning Chuck was in bed
too.

Just like the prior week, we waited as long as
we could. When the house was silent and no light
leaked in under my bedroom door, I slipped out of bed
and through the window.

The five of us met this time at the corner, and we all made the walk back into the woods to John's spot for our first official meeting.

"We're ready," John said. We held a vote and named him the master of ceremonies for this first meeting. It was his baby, after all. He lit the fire, and we took our seats on the logs around the edge of the circle. "Welcome everyone to the first meeting of the Nightmare Club. You all know and understand the rules. Are there any questions about how we will keep score?"

"As long as everyone agrees to be honest, I think this will be a lot of fun," Merrie said. She managed to sit cross-legged even on the felled log, her fingertips played with the dirt as she spoke.

"Agreed," said Chuck.

"Right, right." John said. "We have to promise to be honest. If you have a nightmare that relates to a specific story heard here, you *have* to report it. Otherwise, what's even the point of being here?"

We all nodded. This was all stuff we'd talked about during the week. John was summarizing it because this was an actual meeting, so now it was official.

"Great. Next: names." John pulled off his ball cap, ran a hand through his hair. "So no one has an unfair advantage, we will pull the name of the person telling the story at the beginning of the meeting. The person who tells that story this week will have their name removed when we draw names next week. This process will continue until all five members have gone. Then we will all be entered in the next drawing."

Again, we all nodded.

"Chuck, am I forgetting anything?"

"Anna and I will be in charge of keeping score. If you have a nightmare, report it to one of us, and we'll keep a running tally. Before every meeting we'll read off the scores." Chuck paused, smiled. "This is going to be awesome."

John handed his hat to Chuck and pulled notecards and a pencil out of his back pocket. He handed one notecard to each of us. "Put just your first name on the card and then fold it exactly in half, so we won't know whose card is whose."

I took the pencil first, wrote my name down, folded my card, and passed the pencil to Merrie, who did the same. Marcus went next, then Chuck, and finally John. When we were finished, we dropped our cards in the hat. A light breeze blew, it was warm and felt good against my skin. The fire shifted and danced with the wind and then steadied itself when it stopped. John closed up the hat and shook it a few times.

"Who's going to do the honors?" he asked. "Anna-banana?"

I shook my head, "No, I nominate Marcus."

Marcus had been the quietest of the group and of the five of us, he seemed the least excited about the Nightmare Club. I knew Merrie was excited because it was all she talked about when I saw her. Chuck was the same way. John never hid his excitement for anything well, but I had a tough time getting a read on Marcus. I just wanted him to feel like part of the group. Although, I secretly hoped he wouldn't pull his own name. If he did, I feared it would be a very short inaugural meeting.

"Yeah, I vote Marcus, too," Chuck said.

"Yeah, Marcus," Merrie chimed in.

"Well, I guess it's unanimous," John said, still shaking his hat as he strode over to where Marcus was standing on the opposite side of the fire.

John shook the hat a few more times and, just like we'd all seen teachers do, John lifted it up so it was above Marcus's head. Marcus looked up, smiled, then reached up and grabbed a note card from the pile that sat inside it. John pulled the hat down and backed away.

Marcus turned to the rest of us. "Y'all ready?" he said, his voice quivering.

At first, I thought it was nerves. But I looked around the circle and realized Chuck, Merrie, John, and I were all staring at him, eyes wide, mouths agape. He wasn't nervous, he was enjoying the looks on our faces and simultaneously laughing at us. Maybe we were all taking this thing too seriously and Marcus understood it. Or maybe he was just trying to torment us, but whatever the reason, it was working.

"Yeah, we're ready. Come on!" Merrie said, a smile growing on her face. She stomped the ground with her foot.

"Hold on a second." Marcus played at the edge of the folded card with his thumb like he was going to open it. Then he stopped and looked at us again, his face somber. "You know, I feel like this is a heavy moment and I should say something important right now."

"No, you're good. Just tell us the name." Chuck said.

"Yeah, yeah. You're right." Marcus sucked a breath in and held the card in front of him, ready to pull it open and read the name. Then he stopped and looked around at us again. "I think I have to use the bathroom."

"Oh, Jesus Christ, Marcus!" John laughed.

John strode toward him, but Marcus backpedaled a few steps, laughing along with him. We were all laughing. And the member of the group I had worried wouldn't fit in seemed to have found his place.

"Okay, for real this time," Marcus paused. The giggles around the circle subsided. He opened the card, smiled, then turned the card around for us to see. "It's me."

"Wow. Marcus it is," John said.

John might have assumed the role of leader, it being his baby, but more and more it was becoming clear that it was turning into *our* group. John wouldn't

be the Nightmare Club's leader for much longer. The
club would take on a life of its own. Especially if
Marcus pulled through with a halfway decent story.

"Okay, what are the rules for the story?"
Marcus asked. "Just anything I want, right?"

John looked around at the rest of the group, and
we all nodded.

"I'd say as long as it attempts to give us
nightmares, it doesn't really matter what the story itself
is about," Chuck added.

"Yeah, but please, try to scare us. Honestly, I
could use a little scare tonight. My parents don't ever
let me watch horror movies, so this is the only scary
stuff I'm going to get," Merrie said, wide grin across
her face.

"Well, I'll do my best," Marcus said.

Warm wind whipped through our make-shift
campsite again. This time stronger than the last. It blew
across the top of the metal drum and reduced the size
of the flames, darkening our faces as we sat and
prepared for the first *real* story of the Nightmare Club.
We didn't realize it then, but things had already started
to change.

"Okay," Marcus said, and cleared his throat.
"This is tough going first. I guess, though, I want to
tell you a story that's true. At least it was true when my
cousin told it to me. It happened not that far from here.
We've all been to Chicago before. At least, I assume
we have."

We nodded.

"Well, my cousin, Sean, lives in Chicago—the good part—not the bad parts of the city," Marcus began his story.

Sean used to have to walk home from school every day because both his mom and dad worked. He didn't mind it, and he got to be home by himself after school, which gave him time to relax and be on his own. But he had to walk past this church with a cemetery across the street from it every day. He was an athlete and often had to stay after school for practice. Because of that, when he left school, a lot of times it was already dark out, especially in the fall and winter.

One night he was walking past the church. It was cold out. Not just cold, but freezing—one of the few days a year when it was below zero in the entire Chicago area. He's all bundled up, but still freezing his ass off because of the temperature and the fact his clothes were still damp from sweating at practice. His only thought was about getting home and taking a hot shower. Then he comes up on the church on his left. The wind whipped past him, cutting through his jacket and making him even colder. He had his hands stuffed in his pockets, winter hat on and his zipper pulled up over his nose. The only part of him exposed to the world was his eyes, just enough so he could see. It helped, but only a little because he could still feel the wind and his damp clothes were stiffening, the sweat freezing in the frigid air. As he passed the church—even through the sound of the wind—he heard kids giggling like he was walking by a playground in the middle of summer.

Sean had never seen anyone in the cemetery before. He'd walked by the cemetery hundreds of times over the years on the way home from school and there had never been anyone inside the gates. But on that bitter cold night, he saw three young kids laughing and running around the cemetery. It shocked him, and he stopped in his tracks. Sean still longed for that hot shower, but he couldn't really believe the kids were just playing around in the cold. The entire population of city was moving as fast as they could from one heated place to the next, except those kids.

He watched them for a second or two and realized they weren't bundled up. They had on sweatshirts and jeans, but no winter clothes, no gloves. Sean checked both ways and crossed the street. There were no adults around watching out for the kids, and he was worried about them because of the cold. He got to the other side of the street and pulled open the squeaky metal gate leading into the cemetery. The wind gusted after he walked through the gate and blew it closed behind him with a metallic rattle.

The sound of the gate slamming shut made him jump.

"Hey," Sean yelled at the kids, hoping to grab their attention. They just kept playing, and at first, he thought they were ignoring him. Then the kids scrambled around and hid behind a few of the gravestones. They popped out from behind the stones and started running around giggling and screaming with joy again. None of them said anything. Though, the sounds of their giggles filled his ears.

"I need to get home," Sean said. "But you guys are going to get frostbite or something out here. You should get inside." He turned to leave. He'd tried his best to help them, but he was cold too and if the kids didn't want his help, then he was going to be on his way. And he was still thinking of a hot shower. If he saw a police officer, he would pass along the information about the kids in the cemetery and figured that would be enough to keep him from feeling guilty. As he reached for the metal gate, one of the kids finally spoke.

"Too late," one of the kids said. He turned around and the three kids were just standing there, in a line shoulder to shoulder looking at him.

"You should get inside," Sean repeated his warning. "You don't want frostbite."

"Too late," the middle one said. The kid moved his mouth, but his lips didn't move in time with the words. It was as if the words and the movement of his mouth were two separate things.

"What do you mean too late?" He asked. They didn't reply, just stood there and stared at him. He wanted to go home. but felt responsible for the kids now. If he was standing there talking to them—even if the words didn't make any sense—he had to help them.

Sean moved toward them, put his hand out.

"Come on," he said. "let's get you guys somewhere warm." As soon as he reached for them, his body froze. He couldn't move. People walked by, but no one made a move to help him. He was stuck in place. A coldness moved up his body. It started at his feet and slowly worked its way up his body. The feeling was different than the dry, cold winter air. This coldness felt like death, and it filled him with terror. Sean panicked and turned his attention back to the kids.

The kids weren't moving either. Yet the idea of the four of them—Sean and the three kids—standing in the cemetery unmoving wasn't what bothered him the most about the situation. As he stood watching them, ice moved up their bodies. It started with their feet and moved up their bodies, encrusting them in a thin layer of ice. Sean tried to scream but he still couldn't move. The kids' clothing started to freeze.

Then their bodies began to fall apart, crumbling to pieces where their feet had been only seconds before. He couldn't pull his eyes away as their skin turned black and broke into pieces. He tried again to scream but was still held in place but an unseen force. The kids' bodies had become nothing but frozen dust. Only their faces remained, hanging in the air staring at him, their faces blue, their eyes dark grey ice cubes.

"Too late," a voice echoed around him.

The faces disappeared as did the frozen bodies and clothing that had piled up on the ground. Sean looked around and realized he could move again. He left the cemetery and ran the rest of the way home, barely able to breathe by the time he got there.

Once he got inside his house with the door locked behind him, Sean finally started to calm down. A few minutes later, he was in the shower, warming his cold body. Even though the bathroom was full of steam and the water was turned up as hot as possible, a chill came over him. He shivered.

From somewhere around him, he heard a voice. "Too late."

Marcus stopped talking and for almost a minute the five of us sat in silence. No one really knew what to say or who should break the silence following Marcus's story. It was better than I thought it would be. I had a story in mind in case my name was pulled, but it wasn't nearly as good as the one Marcus had just told. I didn't know if it was real or not, but it felt true at the time. When he was talking, I could see those kids, frozen and falling apart in front of his cousin's eyes.

"Well," John said, finally in a much more somber, subdued tone than he'd had before the story. "I think that wraps up our meeting for the week."

We all stood up, stretching our legs and shaking them out after lifting ourselves up off the low logs. The fire had burned down low in the barrel, so we decided just to leave it as it was. Using our flashlights, we scanned the area to make sure we didn't leave anything behind.

"One last thing," Chuck said. "Marcus will run the meeting next week since he told the story this week. Good luck, Marcus. I hope no one has any nightmares."

"I hope everyone does," Marcus said, a hint of laughter in his voice. "Let's get home. We don't want to be out…too late."

Chapter 3

We'd created the Nightmare Club, but had no idea if the stories we told were ever going to produce nightmares. The whole idea revolved around one—or more than one of us—having nightmares. If there were no nightmares, the club would fall apart pretty quickly. Sure, we all dreamed, but that didn't mean we were going to dream about the one story we heard late on a Saturday night in the middle of the woods. It was an unspoken worry between all five of us, but it didn't take long for us to find out that the Nightmare Club—and it's scoring system—would work.

I was still in bed the morning after the first meeting when I heard Mom's gentle knock on my bedroom door.

"Anna," she said. Her voice was soft, but loud enough that I could hear it through the door and the fan blowing in my face.

I blinked the sleep away a few times and realized I wasn't dreaming, she was talking to me. "Mom." I rubbed my face. "What is it?"

"You friend, Merrie, is here. She's in the living room." The old floor creaked and groaned like it always did when anyone walked across it.

Merrie?

I sat up in bed.

Sunlight poured through my bedroom window which meant it was still early morning. Once the sun got too high in the sky, it missed my window completely. I checked my alarm clock and saw it was just after nine o'clock. We'd got back well after two the night before. Maybe Merrie was just an early riser, but I had a feeling she was there for a specific reason, and I got excited.

I always slept in a tank top, so I threw on a t-shirt and went out to the living room. Merrie sat on our worn sofa, slumped back against it, eyes half open, bags beneath them.

"Merrie, are you okay?" I rushed to sit next to her.

I had an idea why she was there and suppressed a smile as I looked at the exhausted girl. I didn't want to seem too excited by her lack of sleep.

"Yeah, I'm fine. Other than the fact that I barely slept."

"So, you had to come wake me up?" I knocked my knee against hers.

"Well, I waited until nine to knock on your door. Plus, honor system right. I'm supposed to report any…" She looked up at the door for either of my parents, but they were nowhere around. Still, she lowered her voice to a whisper. "Any nightmares."

"You had one?" I was shocked. I hadn't expected for everything to go as planned. But it seemed the Nightmare Club was real.

She nodded.

"That is so great!"

One look at Merrie's tired face told me that was the wrong thing to say, but I couldn't contain my true feelings. This validated everything about the Nightmare Club. It was going to work.

"I mean, I'm sorry you're so tired, but really… You know… For the Club, it's great."

"I get it."

"Wait right here."

I hopped up off the couch and went back down the hall to my bedroom. Chuck and I had made a notebook specifically for the Nightmare Club. We didn't put any details down about the club in case Mom or Dad found it, but we had everyone's name written down. Chuck made a chart to keep track of the scores as well as who had the nightmares. I lifted up my mattress, grabbed the notebook from the box spring, a pencil from my desk, then rejoined Merrie in the living room.

I dropped the notebook on the coffee table, returned to the couch, and leaned forward, flipping the notebook open to the score tracking page. Next to Marcus's name, I carefully placed a single 'X.' Then I flipped to the nightmare page and put an 'X' next to Merrie's name.

"What's that one?" she asked, watching me put the mark next to her own name.

"Oh," I pulled the notebook up to my lap and leaned back against the couch so she could look at it with me. "We made a chart to see who has nightmares the most too. We just thought it would be interesting to keep track of that kind of stuff."

"Like stats?"

"Yeah, sure. Like baseball statistics and other sports. The more information you have, the better. Right?"

Merrie nodded.

"Do you want to tell me what the dream was like? You don't have to. If you just want to go back to bed and try to sleep, I totally understand. You look tired."

"Thanks." Merrie gave a weak smile.

She didn't move or start to talk. I didn't really know what else to say to her, so we just sat in the silence of the house. I heard Mom in the basement doing something, probably switching the laundry. Dad was outside in the yard doing the usual weekend yard work. So, we had the time to ourselves. I figured if she wanted to talk, she would tell me. If she just wanted to go home, she'd tell me that, too. But I was content to let silence rest until she broke it.

She sighed.

I turned toward her, pulling my knee up on the couch so I could look at her.

"I didn't really think it was *that* scary of a story last night, did you?" Merrie said.

"No, not really," I said. It was true, but the atmosphere—being outside in the middle of the night in the woods with the fire going—made it seem a lot scarier than if we'd been sitting outside or in someone's living room telling stories in the middle of the day. "It was a good story. Interesting. But not super scary."

"Right. But the whole walk home and then when I was lying in bed, I just kept having this one image in my head. It wasn't even in the story, but it was part of the story, kinda."

I nodded, and had an idea what she would say.

"When his cousin was in the shower and heard that voice say *'too late.'* That was it. I just couldn't stop picturing him in the shower, standing there trying to warm up and to forget what he saw, and then boom—it all comes back and those ghosts, or whatever they were, are right back there with you again."

"I thought you were going to say that. Chuck and I have been talking a lot lately and have been trying to figure out how to make a story scary, but also stick with you because, if it's scary and you forget about it by the time you're at home in bed, it doesn't really help—" I stopped. The lawn mower started outside and we both looked to the window. I didn't think Dad could hear us, but it was more or less a reminder that both of my parents were around and we didn't want them hearing us. "You want to walk to your house together?"

"Yeah, let's go," Merrie said.

"Give me a minute," I ran to my room and grabbed a pair of socks and slipped my shoes on. I looked in the mirror. My hair was a mess, but I was only going a few streets over to Merrie's house, then I'd be back. I ran my fingers through my hair and gave it a shake, helping it flatten down a little. "Ready."

Merrie was already at the door.

"Mom!" I yelled into the house, knowing she'd hear me. "I'm just walking with Merrie back to her house, then I'll come right home for chores!"

I gave Dad a wave, and he waved back at us as he pushed the lawn mower across the front yard.

"Okay, so what were you saying about scary stories?" Merrie said once we were on the street.

"Just that the story has to be memorable *and* scary. A scary story by itself won't get you any points. You have to have something that will stick with a person. Marcus's story had it—that *too late* thing. He said it a couple of times during the story, and then it was what the cousin heard in the shower. It ended with those words too. Chuck and I have been saying the same thing. I'm not saying that's the only way to do it, but it's one way to make sure the story sticks in someone's head."

"Wow! You guys really did some research on this. I was just going to try to tell a ghost story. I didn't even really plan anything out. I was worried I would get called. Now I know I've got to be ready for next week."

"We didn't really do much research. Just talked about things that we always thought were scary. Chuck is really good at school, especially English and writing and stuff, so I try to listen to what he says."

We turned the corner. A car drove by and we drifted to the shoulder of the road. Once it passed, we moved back over, both walking on the pavement again.

"What else did you come up with? For storytelling, I mean," Merrie said.

We were getting closer to her house, and I made a quick scan of her yard to make sure her parents and even her little sister weren't outside in case they overheard us. No one was there, though. It was just the two of us.

"Not much really. Mostly we talked about what we are going to do. Authors who write scary stories and things like that."

"Did you make a list?"

"No, just a head list. Do you want to meet us at The Field later? I don't know if Marcus is going, but

Chuck and John and me will be there. I'm sure the boys want to talk about last night, too. Maybe we can share story secrets and stuff."

"Yeah, okay," Merrie said, but she sounded unsure, nervous. Her eyes moved back and forth slowly.

"What is it?" I asked.

"Oh, it's stupid," Merrie rubbed her hand against the opposite arm. "Nothing."

"Just tell me," I said, and leaned toward her so my shoulder gently bumped hers.

"I— I just hope I'm not the only one who had a dream last night."

"Don't worry. Trust me, no one will care. They'll probably be more excited about it than anything. Marcus will just make fun of the ones that didn't have a dream, anyway. It will be fine."

"Okay," she smiled, and ran to her house, then turned back. "What time?"

"We'll be there all day. Just try to get some sleep and come later."

I turned toward home and went back into my bedroom. I contemplated going back to sleep, but decided against it. I ate breakfast, showered, and got my chores done before Chuck rolled out of bed. I was just sitting in the living room watching TV when he came in, scratching his head and looking confused.

"How long did I sleep? How long have you been up?"

"A while," I said, answering both of his questions. "But hurry up and get your stuff done so we can get to The Field. I've got some news for you."

His eyes lit up, "Oh? What kind of news?"

"Nope. Get your stuff done, then I'll tell you. Let's go!" I laughed as he grumbled and left to do his chores.

Chapter 4

The name of our neighborhood was Prairie View. I'm not sure how they came up with the name, because not only were there no prairies near us, none of the views were anything other than mediocre at best. The name meant literally nothing, other than that The Field we always found ourselves at was called Prairie View Park.

When we were younger, our parents would take us to the playground where there was a high metal slide, which was good for burning the back of your legs on sunny days. A set of three swings were attached to an A-frame with rusted metal chains, the seats of which were always falling apart. You took your life in your hands every time you decided to swing more than a few feet off the ground.

Finally, there was the merry-go-round—the metal one with the handles welded into it that you have to spin manually. I loved those things when I was

younger, but inevitably, someone fell off and dragged
their legs on the gravel beneath it. They would end up
bleeding for a few days and have to try not to pick the
scabs the rest of the week. When we were younger,
that was the stuff we did for fun.

Prairie View Park also had a few baseball fields
and a tennis court that doubled as a basketball court,
and plenty of wide-open space. It left us with a lot of
things to do on those long summer days. As we got
older, we stopped calling it Prairie View Park and
started calling it The Field. It seemed less kid-like that
way. No one wanted to say 'Hey, I'm going to the park
later,' but going to The Field made it sound more
mature. At least to our early teenage ears.

When we finally made it to The Field that day,
John and Marcus were already there, sitting on the roof
of one of the dugouts, legs swinging over the edge.
Merrie wasn't there yet.

"So," John said the moment we were in ear
shot. "Either of you have dreams last night?"

I hadn't even asked Chuck if he'd had a dream,
assuming he would have told me if he had. I shook my
head no. Chuck did as well.

"What about you two?" Chuck asked.

"Yeah, actually," John said. The corners of his
mouth dropped the slightest bit. I'm sure he didn't
even realize it, but I still saw. Merrie would be happy
to know she wasn't the only one.

"What about Merrie?" Marcus didn't work to hide his grin. "Either of you two talk to her this morning?"

"I did. I think we should wait until she's here to talk, though. That good with everyone?" I looked at each of the boys, and they nodded their agreement.

"I got a basketball," Marcus said. "How about some two-on-two?"

I don't know how long it was that we played before Merrie showed up. Those summer days, time was different. It wasn't like time when we were at school. There was breakfast, lunch, and time to go home for the night. Whenever we talked about time, we always spoke of it in terms of how long until lunch or how many more games we could play before we went home for the night. We were about three games in when we heard her yell at us over the sound of the ball hitting the asphalt.

"Hey," Merrie shouted.

John was dribbling the ball, stopped and held it against his hip. We were all sweating pretty good. John and Marcus had dominated the first two games and were ahead in the third game, so we were all ready for a break in the action.

Merrie held up a large red thermos and a stack of plastic cups.

"That looks amazing," Marcus said. He jogged over to where Merrie stood.

"You don't even know what's inside," Chuck said.

"Yeah, but I can tell it's cold and delicious," Marcus laughed.

"It's hot tomato soup," Merrie said.

"For real?" Marcus's eyes got wide. "It's way too hot for soup today."

"You really think I would bring tomato soup? It's a thousand degrees out here." Merrie laughed. "It's Kool-Aid."

"Let's go over there in the shade." John pointed to a small group of trees with thick grass beneath them.

We usually sat in the shade when we needed a break from the sun. The five of us migrated over there, and Merrie poured ice-cold red Kool-Aid into plastic cups. As we drank, a silence fell over the group, and I felt all eyes turn to me.

"I guess we should give an update then, now that we're all here," I said. I stopped to gulp down the rest of my Kool-Aid. I flashed Merrie a quick look, hoping she caught it, then looked over to John. "John, you had a nightmare, right?"

"Ah, yeah. I did."

"Do you want to tell us about it? We never really discussed that or anything," Chuck said. "But perhaps it makes sense for the people who had nightmares to tell us what they remember, if there is anything about them that they *do* remember."

"Yeah. Yeah, sure. I'm fine with sharing," John said.

"Everyone else cool with that? With always sharing the dreams we have, if and when we have them?" Chuck looked around.

We all agreed.

"It's a rule then," John said. "Merrie, did you have a nightmare too?"

She nodded.

"Okay. Well, I'll go first. Unless you want to?"

"No. Go ahead." Merrie smiled. I could see the relief on her face.

"Okay. All right. So, I mean, it wasn't even that much really. But I definitely had a nightmare, because I woke up and my heart was, like, racing and shit. It was, you know, like really beating fast. I don't remember a whole lot of it. There was this guy there—tall, skinny. He's just standing there, and I can't see his face, only the outline of the hat or something on his head. Anyway, he doesn't say anything, just is standing there. And then the dream just switches to the kids from Marcus's story. And just like the tall guy, they don't say anything and I can't see their faces. But I can see their eyes and they're just staring at me, and their bodies just start to disintegrate, like in the story. Next thing I know, I wake up in bed, sweating. I laid there for a bit and eventually fell back asleep. And that's, well, that's all there is."

"Wow! I can't believe my story caused a dream like that. Gotta admit, it's kinda awesome!" Marcus said.

John rubbed his fingernails against the side of his face, like I'd seen him do a hundred times before. I always thought it reminded me of something a guy with a beard would do, but John was still two or three years away from growing a beard.

"What about you Merrie?" Chuck asked.

John took off his hat and ran his hand through his hair, which he did even more often than rubbing the side of his face. He looked nervous.

Merrie recounted her dream. When she mentioned the part about remembering the kids saying 'too late,' Chuck shot me a look and gave me a wink. We were on the same page with that one.

When she was done, I felt like it was my turn to speak.

"So that's it, right? No other dreams? I didn't have one."

"Me neither." Chuck shrugged.

"So the score as of right now, is Marcus with two and the rest of us with zero. Remember, we agreed that if anyone has a nightmare related to Marcus's story, even if it's after today, it still counts as a point for Marcus and must be reported to either Anna or myself," Chuck said. He was using his *proper* voice that was usually reserved for practicing presentations for school

"Also," I chimed in, "Chuck and I made another chart to keep track of who has the most nightmares, so that way we know who gets nightmares from which people. For example, we'll keep track of the fact that John and Merrie had nightmares from Marcus's story. That way, if the next time Marcus tells a story they have nightmares again, we'll know that, for whatever reason—"

"John and Merrie are more likely to have a nightmare if I tell the story. Really cool. I like it," Marcus said with a nod.

"Exactly," Chuck said.

We each recounted our nights before we parted ways. Chuck and I described the story of sneaking back into our house. Marcus and Merrie told a similar version at their own house. John was the only one who was able to just walk in through the front door.

"It makes it way easier to sneak out since my room got moved to the basement last year. I can basically just come and go as I please because they are upstairs asleep and I'm in the basement by myself. They don't even know, really, when I wake up or go to bed. They just tell me to get some sleep and then trust that I actually do it. If I get caught, though," John said with a laugh, "I'll have to move back upstairs and share a room with my little brother again. That would suck!"

We all laughed, and the overall mood lightened.

With all five of us there, we couldn't play two-on-two basketball anymore and no one wanted to figure out how to adapt a three-person game to a five-person game. Instead, we relaxed and talked under the tree for the rest of the afternoon.

Other than Marcus mentioning the fact that he was winning in an example of perfect teenage trash-talk, no one mentioned the dreams for the rest of the day. In fact the topic of Nightmare Club was hardly spoken of for the rest of the week.

Chuck was quiet during the walk home and that night, when we sat and watched TV. He was usually talkative and I could tell he was formulating a story in his head, though he never told me outright. When it was just the two of us, I knew he ached to have his name called on Saturday night so he could tell his story and rack up a few points. Maybe even take the lead in the Nightmare Club competition. Before we knew it, it was Saturday night, and we were standing as a group again, at the corner, about to head back into the woods for the second official meeting of the Nightmare Club.

Chuck led the way this time down the street. John, who usually walked with Chuck, fell back from the lead a little bit and settled in next to Merrie and me. Marcus sped up and walked stride for stride with Chuck.

"Anna-banana." John put an arm around my shoulder and gave me a brother-like side-hug. "Who do you want to have their name pulled tonight?"

"Who do I want? Or who do I think?"

"Why not both?"

"I want it to be you, John," Merrie said.

"Well, being totally honest… I *know* Chuck has been figuring out a story in his head since last week. I have a feeling it's going to be pretty good, so I want it to be him. But I still feel like this whole group is your baby, John, so I also think it's going to be you. And I'd be happy either way." I reached out and slid my arm into his, locking our elbows, then smiled at Merrie, who did the same on his other side.

"Well, I hope it's me, too," John said. "Come on ladies! I'll show you the way!"

We laughed and walked arm in arm down the streets a few steps behind Chuck and Marcus. It was strange to be just marching down the middle of the street at this time of night. It was only the third time we'd done this—second for Marcus and Merrie—but we'd already gone from sneaking down the streets at night, hoping no one saw us, to laughing and joking arm in arm, stretched out almost the width of the road. We didn't have a care in the world. I didn't mind being silly. We all knew that once we got to the meeting place, things would take a somber turn.

Chapter 5

Our second meeting started pretty much the same as the first one did, except we didn't go over the rules as much. Everyone knew them by now, anyway. We were all experts by that point.

I reviewed the scores and asked once more if anyone had any more dreams about Marcus's story since that first night. No one had. Marcus ran the meeting in pretty much the same way John did the week before. When it was time to pick a name from the hat, he chose Merrie to pull the name. We all sat in a nervous silence, excited but quiet as she reached up and drew the name from above her.

"If she pulls her own name like Marcus did, it's going to get even creepier than it already is," John said.

Merrie held the paper, still folded in half in front of her. Marcus had made a joke of it the week before, but Merrie didn't joke. She did, however, make sure the tension lasted a while before finally opening the paper and looking down at it. A smile crossed her face, and I knew from that reaction alone that there could only be two names on that note card: hers or John's.

"Oh, come on," I said. "Don't leave us in suspense, Merrie. What does it say?"

"It's John." She spun the card around and held it out to the rest of us.

"Oh, I was hoping for this," Marcus said, rubbing his hands together.

Chuck looked disappointed. Whatever he'd been preparing, it was going to be good when we finally heard it. The more time he had to improve the story, the better—and scarier—it would be.

"Here we are." John stood close to the burning can, his usual, joking grin gone.

Comparing him to the guy I'd walked arm in arm with down the road not ten minutes earlier, he seemed like a different person. The flames threw up strange, dancing shadows on his face, yet his eyes were veiled in darkness somewhere below the brim of his baseball hat. The only way I knew his eyes were even there was the small glint of light reflecting off his pupils. Everything else was dark, black.

John took off his baseball hat, ran a hand through his hair, replaced the hat, and began.

"Marcus told us a true story last week. We think it was true, anyway," John said, and our circle, the woods, the world, went silent. "We think it was true because his cousin told him the story. I don't think Marcus would lie to us. I believe his cousin told him that story. But I have to be honest here, Marcus. I don't know your cousin, so I have a hard time judging that story. Maybe that story was based on a true story. That doesn't make it true though. My story isn't based on a true story. This story isn't a story that happened to someone else that I know. It *is* however, a true story. I know it's true because it happened to me."

There was something different about John's voice. It was hypnotizing. His tone went up and down. The words flowed out of his mouth like water down a drain, spiraling down and pulling us with it, sending us into something like a trance.

"We sit here every Saturday night telling scary stories. The point of these stories is to give others nightmares. It's a perfect place for it, isn't it? There's a can set up for us to light a fire so we can see. Logs laying perfectly across the ground for us to sit on in a circular pattern. We're far enough away from the road and the houses that no one can see or hear us. And it's late, so we can get here without a single soul knowing we're here. Our parents, our younger brothers and sisters—everyone who knows us—thinks we're at home, in bed, asleep, waiting for Sunday morning to come so we can walk down to The Field and spend another day playing or shooting the shit. Basically doing whatever we want, like we've done all summer. But we're not there. We're not at home, safe in our beds. We're here, in the woods at night, telling dark stories with the hope of producing nightmares in the people who hear them."

I looked at John, watching the place where I knew his eyes were, but still didn't see them until he paused. The rhythmic droning of his voice had stopped, and so did the trance. That was a great opening, and he'd obviously practiced it. He was setting a mood, which was something Marcus hadn't done. This story was going to be much different.

"We came here—Chuck, Anna-banana, and I— a couple weeks ago. When we did, we knew we wanted to ask Marcus and Merrie to join us. But also, when we were here, Chuck or Anna—I'm sorry I don't remember who it was—but one of them asked me how I knew this was here. Whether I had set this up on my own. I heard the question back then, but chose to ignore it. Sorry to whoever it was that asked. I wasn't ready to tell this story then. I am now."

He walked out from behind the fire so he passed by us, his feet inches from ours as he made a lap around the flaming barrel. He then resumed his position behind the fire, again looming over us. Shadow and light danced across his face.

"I wasn't ready because, to be honest, I'm not exactly sure how I found this place. But I'll fill you in best I can. And, since I'm opening up so completely here, if anyone decides after hearing all of this that they don't want to be a part of this club anymore, I completely understand. If you choose to leave us, you will still be my friend, and I will still see you at The Field every day. You just won't come to this meeting, and I'm fine with that."

Chuck puffed some air out of his nose at that. I could understand it; John was obviously saying all of this extra stuff for effect. Chuck wasn't buying it, but for whatever reason, I believed what John was saying. This felt more like a confession than a story. Maybe he was just a good actor.

John noticed the snort, but said nothing. He just tilted his head toward Chuck, smiled with the left side of his mouth, and continued on.

"It was about three weeks ago, I guess, now. It was when I first got the idea for this club, actually. Before I said anything to Chuck or Anna. It was just a half-baked idea I had in my head of something we could do at night that would be fun and maybe a little spooky and give us another chance to keep score. God knows we can't do much without having a winner and a loser. I simply woke up one morning and had this Nightmare Club idea, and I kind of already knew exactly how it would work; telling the stories and keeping track of the number of nightmares each story produced. Pretty much the way we set it up. But I didn't want to go to you guys without having a spot where we could do it. Scary stories told in the middle of the day don't really have the same impact as those told at night, so we needed some place to go at night. I just didn't know where.

"We couldn't do it at someone's house because we each have a curfew. If we were older, maybe we could get away with being out late, but not yet. So, we had to find a place away from everyone. Away from the neighborhood. Away from The Field, because you all know how many people keep their eyes on that place after dark. I figured I'd come out here in the woods, find a spot, and then get Anna-banana and Chuck to come with me to get it set up for our weekly meetings. I told you guys I had a doctor's appointment that morning, but I was really just coming out here into the middle of nowhere during the day to find us a spot. And I found this place."

John paused again. For such a fantastic opening, the story was kind of dragging. I didn't really feel like he was doing anything other than telling us what he did. Maybe it would get better, but I was losing hope.

"But it didn't look like this. The clearing was here. The trees all around us were here, but this area, for whatever reason, was free from any tall trees. There were a few small ferns and stuff, but the area was pretty much just clear. I looked in each direction and couldn't see any houses, which meant, most likely, that they couldn't see me. I'd have to come back at night to double check, but I thought it would be perfect, assuming I could find a place for us to sit and build a fire-pit that would work.

"I looked around but couldn't find any rocks to build a pit or anything to use for seating. If I wanted any of those things, I would have to bring them in from somewhere else. So, that morning when I found this place, I left here knowing I'd come back at night. That night, by myself—just like we've all done the past few weeks—I sneaked out of my house at around one in the morning, flashlight in hand, and I came here.

"It was actually really easy to find in the dark, and I knew I'd be able to repeat the process again leading you all with me. But when I got here, the trees had been toppled over and the barrel—filled with branches and twigs—sat in the middle of this circle in the same position it's in now. I was shocked to see it the way it was, because the trees—as you can see— aren't cut down. They were blown down or pulled down like in a storm or something. But it hadn't been stormy that day at all. I didn't know how they could have fallen like that.

"I shined my flashlight around to see if there was some sign as to how the damage occurred, but I couldn't see much of anything. As I stood here, pretty much in the exact spot I'm standing in right now, I realized it was set up perfectly for how we needed it— logs to sit on, a barrel to act as a fire pit in the middle. I didn't know how it happened, but it was perfect. My next thought was that I just had the wrong spot, that the real place I'd scoped out earlier in the day was a hundred yards further into the woods and I just missed this place the first time through. But something inside me told me it wasn't. This was the same place, just…transformed."

John looked around at us, and then continued on with his story.

"'Well, hello,' a voice said from behind me. I jumped a mile and fell down over that tree you're sitting on Marcus." John pointed at him, then walked over behind him and turned to look into the darkness beyond, where the light of the shrinking flames couldn't reach.

Him saying that made me jump, because the voice John had made was one altogether different from any voice I'd heard him make before. It was low and deep and scratchy, as if it wasn't his.

"'Who are you?' I asked, and waved my flashlight in the direction the voice came from. At first, I couldn't see anyone, like the voice had just come from nowhere. As I got back up to my feet, the light of the flashlight just managed to catch part of his hand. I had swept past him with the light and had to swing it back before I finally settled on the hand again. I moved my light around until I found the rest of him. He towered above me; his face hidden in darkness.

"'Who are you?' I asked again. This time I was breathless, feeling actual fear of this guy who should not have been here. I took a step back and tried my best to keep the light on his chest, his face, but he remained covered by shadows. He was tall. Not impossibly so. Not inhuman. But a really tall basketball player height. Taller than most people. But he was thin. Too thin to ever think about playing basketball. I couldn't see much of his clothes, other than that they were dark and, on his head, he wore one of those hats. You know those old-fashioned ones, like a top hat."

John paused and stepped back over the fallen tree, this time moving just behind me. I looked up at him until he stopped moving. I didn't want to crane my neck up, so I just watched the fire and listened to his story. And then I remembered that he mentioned this same guy a week before when he told us about the nightmare he had from Marcus's story. He must have thought the guy in his dream was creepy enough to include in a story. Since he already told us about it, it took away from the creepiness of his story though.

"'Why, John,'" John said in the voice that was not really his. "'I'm here to help you. I already *have* helped you, young man. If you can believe it.'

"'Why would you help me out here in the middle of the night. You can just leave okay. I don't need your help,' I said.

"'But you do need my help, John. You do need it. You want to bring your friends here. You want to tell them stories and give them nightmares. And I want to help you with that. In order to do all of those things, you need a place. I have been so nice as to provide a location for you and your friends. So please, come here, use this place, tell your stories. But most of all, give them nightmares. The more, the better.' The scarecrow-like man said.

"'I just had the thought of this today. I haven't even told anyone about this,' I said.

"'You didn't really think I was just like any other person, did you?'

"I shook my head," John said. "Still holding the light on his chest, I could see the shadow of his head, but still couldn't see his face. He stood about where I am now."

John put his hands on my shoulders. I tried to shrink away from his touch but I couldn't. And he was cold. So cold.

"'Look at my face, John,' he said, then kind of stepped toward me so he was almost right in front of me, just towering over me, looking down at me and I stared up at him.

"'Look at me!'

"I kept the light pointed down but looked up at him.

"'No, see my face, and you will understand.'

"'No,' I whimpered like a little fucking baby. 'Please don't make me.'"

Again, I was shocked at how John was able to change his voice to match what was happening in the story. It was John speaking in the story, but he was

crying, begging for his life. His whine, the pleading, it
sounded nothing like him. It sounded, perhaps, like he
might have sounded that day, with this man standing
over him.

"He just loomed over me. It was like he grew
taller because I kept looking up, up, up at him until it
seemed like he was twelve feet tall.

"'See my face now!' His voice was not human.
The words were garbled, like his throat was filled with
phlegm as he spoke.

"I started crying. I lifted the light to his face,
and I pissed myself.

"I-I can't even really remember what his face
looked like. As soon as I saw it, I dropped to my knees,
and passed out. Right here in the dirt. I don't know
where he went, but he was gone. I woke up drooling,
my pants wet with piss, sometime later that night. The
man was gone, but I knew his secret. I saw, right
before I lost control of my body… I saw what he
wanted me to see. He wasn't really a man. Wasn't a
person, at least not the way we think of them, anyway.
But he wasn't like a ghost or demon, either. He was
something else. But he fed off of nightmares. He needs
our nightmares to stay alive. So, he wanted us to set up
this group here, in this place because it gives him that
many more nightmares to feed upon. I didn't answer
the question of how I knew this area was here, because
I didn't know how it got set up. We needed a place to
hold the Nightmare Club meetings, and I guess he

wanted to help us out. Because he did help us, and now we will help him.

"I-I learned one more thing about this guy, this *thing* before I passed out. I'm not sure how I know all this; it was like he just drilled into my brain when I saw his face. But, anyway… He wants to be called Mr. Nightmare."

We didn't know if John was done telling his story, so silence hung in the air as we processed what we'd just heard. I thought, probably the others did, that the entire story was an elaborate re-telling of how we ended up here as a group. But something about John's face, something about his voice, something about the way he told the story, made it feel real. Even though he'd mentioned Mr. Nightmare last week, I wasn't sure what to think.

No one spoke.

The fire had burned low enough in the barrel that we could just leave it. So we turned on our lights, scanned the area for anything we might have dropped, then left through the trees.

The walk back was mostly silent—a few low whispers between Marcus and Chuck, and that was it. Merrie walked next to me the whole way back to the corner, but we never said a word to each other. John led us out, and no one even tried to talk to him.

John stopped at the corner and looked back at the rest of us. His head was down and he didn't make eye contact with anyone as we approached him.

"Well," Chuck said, when no one else was willing to break the silence. "Night."

"Night," we all said, then turned our separate ways.

"What are you thinking?" I asked Chuck when we were far enough from the others so that they couldn't hear.

"I don't know what to think," Chuck said, matter of fact. "If I hadn't seen his face and just heard him tell the story, I'd assume it was no different from Marcus last week. Just a story that he tried like hell to make feel real. Hell, he described Mr. Nightmare to us last week when he told us about his nightmare. He must have thought that dream was pretty scary, so he just elaborated on it. But Anna, I think he *believes* that happened. If it was an act, then my best friend for over ten years is the greatest actor I've ever seen and I had no idea."

"Yeah. I thought the same thing."

We walked a few steps in silence.

Chuck sighed. "Well, I guess we'll have to see what happens tonight and then talk to him tomorrow."

I didn't say anything as we crept into our yard.

"Night," I whispered as I put my hands on the window sill of my room.

Chuck stayed behind me to make sure I got in okay and then went down to his room.

I was in bed within five minutes.

When I slept, I had a nightmare.

Chapter 6

When we met the next day down at The Field, the
Nightmare Club had a new leader on the scoreboard.
All of us—John included—had dreams of Mr.
Nightmare the previous night. John's nightmare didn't
count toward the overall scores, but it was still
interesting to note that we all had dreams and they
were all very similar.

For me, the dream involved Mr. Nightmare
standing over me in much the same way he stood over
John in his story. But it was day time in my dream.
Because of that I could see his face. Parts of it were
falling off, and I could see the blood and sinew that
lurked beneath his skin. Other parts of his face weren't
falling off, but under the skin a mass of worms crawled
and slid against each other, trapped inside. I screamed,
but when I opened my mouth, no sound came out. I
stared at him, unable to look away. That's not entirely
true, I could turn my head. But when my gaze shifted,
Mr. Nightmare's face was still right there in front of

me, his mouth open, yelling. Dripping blood and slithering worms just inches from my face.

Everyone's nightmare's involved Mr. Nightmare's face. We all saw our own version of it. Our own interpretation of a face that would do the things John described. Before we went down to The Field, Chuck speculated that was John's plan, by not telling us anything about his face but telling us how awful it looked, John made our minds create the face in our sleep.

When I told him I'd dreamed about the face too, Chuck began to think maybe John really had just been acting the night before. That he did a really good job of setting up the story. By not making it too crazy and with the right kind of acting, he'd made us question whether it was real or not. In doing that, he'd told a relatively simple story that scared the shit out of us and accomplished the goal of giving us all nightmares.

I think we all watched John closely that morning. No one asked him right away if the story was true or made up, but I had a feeling Chuck would ask by the end of the day. Maybe when it was just the two of them. The extra scrutiny we all paid John was obvious, but no one said anything about it, including John.

"All right," John said when the sun was past midway through the sky meaning it was probably around one o'clock. "I'm getting hungry. Anyone else hungry?"

My stomach was telling me the same thing. "I'm starving."

Everyone else said they were hungry too.

"Awesome. How about this?" John donned his Master of Ceremonies hat as usual. "I've got hot dogs in my fridge, and my dad taught me how to turn on the grill and stuff the other day. Let's go back to my house, and I'll grill up the hot dogs. We can eat out on my back porch."

"I'm not sure, John. Anna and I are supposed to be only at The Field," Chuck answered for me.

Typical. I would have said yes.

"I'm in," Marcus said.

"Yeah, me too." Merrie said, joining the group.

I gave Chuck a look, raised my eyebrows, and smiled at him. "Yeah, me too."

"Anna-banana's in. Come on, Chuckie. It's on the way to your house. If they ask—which they won't—just tell them you stopped there on your way home. Deal?"

John was the only person in the world who could call him Chuckie. When he was younger, everyone called him Chuckie. As he got older, he hated it more and more.

Chuck considered this.

I remember one morning when I left my room and said good morning to the person I'd only ever

known as Chuckie and he politely told me not to call
him that any more. It was just Chuck from then on.
When we got in fights—which still happened from
time to time, even though we seemed joined at the
hip—I'd always call him Chuckie, just to give him that
extra little jab. I'd also call him Charlie and Charles—
like from *Charles in Charge*—because he hated those
names just as much.

But with John it was different. We'd known
John in the 'Chuckie' days. When John said it, it
wasn't out of malice, like when I used it. It was more
of an endearing term that only a best friend would say.
So, when he used it, it wasn't to mock the fact that
Chuck didn't want to go to his house. It was John's
way of reminding Chuck that they were best friends,
and he should *want* to go grill hot dogs and shoot the
shit on John's back porch.

"Fine," Chuck finally said, like we all knew he
would.

John led the way to his house being his normal,
loud and crazy self. I saw no signs of the terrified kid
who told us about pissing himself in the middle of the
woods the night before. We got to his house and he
had us all sit on the porch while he got lunch ready. He
looked older somehow standing at the grill, tongs in
one hand turning the hot dogs when they needed to be
turned. It was something I'd seen my dad do many
times over the years, but that was my dad. Dads were
supposed to do stuff like grill hot dogs. John was my

friend, and he was doing something only adults did. We were all getting older, I guess. John, Chuck, and Marcus would be in high school come September. I was one year behind them; a soon to be a high-schooler myself. And Merrie, though a year behind me in school, was the same age as me.

We each got two hot dogs in buns with any toppings you could want. I had just mustard on mine, but everyone had their favorites. John played host, getting drinks and plates and napkins like we were real people and not just a group of kids. When we were done, we all sat on the back porch, in the shade of the large oak that filled John's backyard. We were pretty full, and no one wanted to move. Not even Chuck.

"Just pray you don't get Mrs. Jones," Marcus said between laughs, as the older boys were going through the list of eighth grade teachers at school I should try to avoid and why.

"What's wrong with her?" I asked, genuinely curious. "I've seen her in the halls before, and she seems so nice and is always smiling. Is she really mean?"

Chuck, John, and Marcus shared a look and they all smirked.

"What is it?" I said, trying my best not to join in the smirking.

"Come on. You have to tell her. Tell both of us," Merrie said. Us girls were outnumbered, so we had to stick together.

"All right, all right, all right," Marcus said. "So, you're right, Anna; she is nice. Really cool and normal, and everyone likes her. Then, this one day, a few kids stayed after school… I wasn't there, but one of the guys I played baseball with last spring was there. I saw him at practice right after this happened. Anyway, he was there for extra help. His parents both worked and our practice was at the school field, so instead of going home and then coming back, he just stayed and got extra help from his teachers. She was there with him and another kid. She was going over some of the math homework problems on the board and she dropped the chalk on the floor. She could have grabbed another piece off the tray, he said, but instead she bent down to pick up the piece she dropped. When she bent over, she ripped the loudest fart he'd ever heard."

Marcus could barely get the words out, laughing more as the story went on. John and Chuck giggled the whole time.

"Oh, come on," I said, laughing. But I also felt kind of bad. "Everyone does it."

"Yeah, yeah, Anna-B. Everyone does it. But just picture her in your head, bending over…" John stood up and bent over to give me the visual. "And then she rips one. Not just any one, but the loudest fart you've ever heard." Then John put his hand against his mouth to make a fart noise.

All five of us were cracking up. Merrie sat next to me holding her stomach. It wasn't *that* funny of a story, but when you get around a group of friends and everyone is laughing, sometimes it's hard not to laugh. And even harder to stop.

Eventually, though, we all managed to catch our breath and calm down. A silence hung over us, but it was altogether different than what we'd experienced the night before. The night before it had been ominous, full of dread. This silence was friendly, warm, open.

Until Chuck changed it.

"There's some crazy teachers in the middle school for sure, but you girls are going to be fine. I'm sure of it. Before long, we'll all be in the high school together. What do you think the score of the Nightmare Club will be when Merrie is in high school with us?"

"I don't know. I hope we're still doing it then, though," Marcus said.

"Yeah," Chuck said. He looked at John, and I saw my brother's face change. "John, I don't know if anyone else asked you this yet or not, but I just have to. I mean, obviously you made the story up last night, but did you take acting classes or something? Because I sure as hell believed you the whole time. I probably know you better than anyone on earth and I honestly didn't even recognize you last night. But for real, acting classes?"

Chuck tried to keep it light, but his face was more serious. He wasn't angry, just curious. When he gets that look, he needs to have the answer—needs to have the truth. I watched John for a reaction, a tell that would give me more insight into what he was thinking. But when Chuck asked the question, John's face never changed.

"Chuck. Guys. I wasn't fucking around last night. I told you that, and I meant it." John sounded serious. Not like the night before, but it wasn't the same as when he was talking about grilling hot dogs or teachers passing gas either.

"What do you mean?" Chuck said.

"I mean, just what I'm saying, Chuckie. I know it's hard to believe. I'm not mad at you for not believing me. It was messed up. But I saw him. I really saw him there. Mr. Nightmare. It happened just like I said it did. I was obviously telling a scary story, but last night wasn't about the club or anything else. It was about coming clean to you guys. I felt guilty bringing you guys there like that without you knowing how it all came to be. Honest." John put his hands up, palms facing us and leaned back. "I wouldn't— I *couldn't* make that shit up. I don't know if Marcus made his story up or if he really heard it from his cousin, but that story was way better than what I could have come up with. I'm not bullshitting you guys, honestly."

"You really saw that scary, scarecrow like guy with a top hat in the woods? His face was so scary that you passed out in the middle of the night, pissed yourself, and then never wanted to tell us about it?"

I wasn't trying to sound harsh, but I really did want to understand. If there was a crazy guy running around the woods at night sneaking up on kids, we needed to know if it was really true. Especially since we were hanging out in those woods every Saturday night.

"Anna-banana, Chuck, everyone, listen. Look at my face." John looked us each in the eyes, his face serious, stern. "I didn't make the story up. It was true when it happened. It was true when I told you about it last night. And it's true right now."

I still didn't believe he was telling the truth. In the back of my head, I kept remembering that if we all had more nightmares about Mr. Nightmare, or any part of John's story, he would get more points. Maybe he was just keeping up the act because he wanted more points. John was the most competitive of all of us. If anyone would work their story as much as possible, it would be him. Besides, he wasn't the one who brought it up again. Chuck had. John just took the opportunity to keep the story alive. If he admitted the story was made up, it would ruin his chances of getting more points.

Another silence.

We looked at each other, each of us studying him, looking for something that would tell us whether or not the story was actually true.

"I don't know what to say," Chuck said, and threw up his hands. "In the end, without seeing this guy for real, we'll never know for certain if the story was real or not. You know?"

"Yeah, there's always going to be a part of us that wonders," Marcus said. "Just so you all know about my story… My cousin told me parts of it, but I added quite a bit though. You know, I mean, I had to, right?" He flashed a smile, lightening the mood.

"That's the point," Merrie said.

"So what part was real then?" I asked.

"Oh, just like, a little bit was true." Marcus laughed.

"How little?" John said, seemingly happy the spotlight was off him for the time being.

"You know. My cousin, does live in the city. Honest. He really did walk home from school after practice. And there is a cemetery he went by on his way home. And uh…well, you know… I also made up some parts of the story, like I said." Marcus tried to stop himself from smiling but he couldn't.

"So basically, you just used your cousin as a character and the rest of it you just made up?" I was laughing too.

"Yeah. Well, and the cemetery."

The heaviness that was the discussion about John's story and Mr. Nightmare was gone. We laughed about Marcus's story and talked about the differences between middle school and high school. Not that any of us had any actual experience in high school yet. But it was only a few more weeks before the guys would start football practice for the high school freshmen team. I hoped not much would change with our group once they started going to practice without Merrie and I, but there was no way to tell.

We never went back to The Field that day. We sat on John's back porch. His parents worked weekends and were both gone the whole day. The sun was getting low in the sky when we decided to call it a day, so we said our goodbyes and headed off towards our houses. Chuck, Merrie, and me went one way, and Marcus the other. When Merrie turned off toward her house, Chuck looked over at me.

"What do you think?" he asked as soon as Merrie was out of earshot.

I knew what he was talking about, but played dumb. I wanted to see where his head was at before telling him my thoughts. "About what?"

"Come on… John's story. He's just looking to get a few more nightmares out of it, playing it up again like it was real. *No way* there's some tall guy roaming around the woods pulling down trees and dragging barrels around. No way it's true."

"Yeah, I don't really believe it, either. But all that stuff was there. How else would it get there?"

"Are you serious?" Chuck stopped walking for a moment and put a hand on my shoulder.

"What?" I stopped with him. I shot him a look and then kept walking, leaving him a few steps behind me.

Chuck waited while I pulled ahead and then picked up his pace to walk with me once again. "Anna, listen… I'm surprised as hell we haven't run into any older kids out there yet."

"What do you mean?"

"They go out there to drink and get high and stuff. Come on. For real? You don't know what I'm talking about?"

"No, Chuck. I really don't. Please explain." I was getting annoyed.

Chuck obviously knew—or thought he knew—something I didn't and he wasn't really being very open about it. He did that sometimes. It was very 'older brother' of him. And I hated when he played that role.

"Well, obviously, if you want to drink and you're underage, you can't just drink or smoke weed on the back porch with your parents in the living room watching TV. So, if they go on a trip for the weekend—great, you can have people over your house and get wasted. But if they aren't going anywhere, then you have to find a place where no one will catch you and you can spend your time doing whatever illegal activities you want. So, kids go out into the woods, start a fire, and drink or smoke or whatever. I'm positive that's what the area was used for. The only thing I can't explain is the lack of beer cans, roach clips, and condoms. But I bet if we looked at the bottom of the metal drum, we'd find all of that shit."

"Okay, well I didn't know all that, but whatever. I guess the point is you don't believe him. I don't really believe him. It's a little too convenient. I don't get why he kept the story going, either."

"I do. And I know you do, too. John is a great friend, and I would count on him to have my back when it really mattered. But this is just a game. He'll do whatever he can to win at baseball or basketball or any other sport. When we're keeping score, it's fair to say he doesn't care about friendship during the game, right? He takes the shortcuts and does what he can to win, as long as it's within the rules. He's the most competitive person we know."

"Yup." I nodded.

"So, knowing that, and knowing that any dream we have this week about Mr. Nightmare gives him more points…"

"He's going to do whatever he can to win." I finished Chuck's thought for him.

"Exactly. I can't say I won't have another dream about that damn story, because he did a great job of telling it. But there's no way I believe any of that stuff. It's just part of the story. Part of the game."

I nodded. By that time we'd made it home.

Our porch light was on, which meant mom was making dinner, so we'd made it just in time. Before Chuck even pulled open the screen door, I caught the smoky scent of meat charring on the grill. Mom wasn't cooking dinner after all.

We entered and went right into the kitchen.

"Hey guys," Mom said. "Your dad is cooking on the grill tonight. Stick your heads out and let him know if you want hot dogs or hamburgers."

Chuck and I shared a look, and Dad stuck his head in through the back door. "Burgers or dogs tonight, kids?"

"Burgers," we both said.

<u>Chapter 7</u>

By the end of the summer, we'd each had a chance to tell one story. I was the last to go, on the final weekend of summer. It was bittersweet. The five of us had become inseparable over those six weeks, and we'd had a lot of fun times together. The Nightmare Club was part of it, but not all of it. Though, I think having that secret between us, the five of us, made us that much closer. When I saw Marcus, John, or Merrie somewhere where there were other people around, even if I just caught their eye, for the rest of our lives, there would be this secret between us. It made us closer as a group. However, the scores at the end of the first round were disappointing, unless your name was John Workman.

The following afternoon, we had hot dogs at John's house. There'd been two more dreams by Marcus about our friend, Mr. Nightmare, adding those to John's first night total of four. He ended up with six points. Chuck was in second place with three and

Merrie, Marcus, and I were all tied with two. Not the showing I'd wanted, but Chuck was rather happy with his total, mostly because he told a regular old scary story. He didn't try to make us believe it was a true story or do a lot of acting like John had done. Chuck's story was just that, a story, but it was scary as hell. He and John were the only ones to give me nightmares.

We knew once school started back up, we'd be seeing less of each other, but made a promise to continue our meetings. They might not happen every week, we realized, but we'd do our best. Even if it meant moving the meeting to Friday nights, or even Sunday nights, if it was the only time we could all get there. We all wanted to do it and would make time for it.

Mr. Nightmare was never mentioned again after the final nightmare John's story produced. No one brought it up, and I think everyone was happy about it. It was nice to just be with my friends and not have to worry about the strange 'was it true or not true' story John told. I was happy not thinking about Mr. Nightmare. Unfortunately, that only lasted until the middle of October, in the middle of the woods, when John's name was pulled again.

The leaves were, for the most part, off the trees and piled up on the ground. We had to wade our way through them that night. It reminded me more of walking through a foot of snow after a storm in January than a snowless night in mid-October. While the night was mild—not cold like some of our more recent meetings had been—the lack of leaves provided a new and interesting challenge.

Over time, the meeting spot became known to us as The Nightmare Dwelling—and later just The Dwelling. With the insulation of the leaves gone, sound carried a lot further. We could hear sounds of the semi-trucks on the interstate, which was more than five miles away. And cars passing by on smaller roads nearby. Knowing sound travelled different in the fall, we lowered our voices for the rest of the night. We also tried to keep our steps soft because, to our ears, the crunch of leaves underfoot was the loudest sound in the woods.

When John stood in front of us for the first time since his Mr. Nightmare story, his voice, his face, everything about him changed. It was instantaneous.

"I'm glad my name was pulled tonight," he said.

His face was longer than usual. His mouth, usually pregnant with a smile, was downturned. His eyes nearly lifeless. I didn't know how he was able to portray such a dramatic change in such a short period of time, because he'd been his normal self on the walk over.

"I was honestly going to ask you guys if you didn't mind staying back with me after the story so I could tell you this if my name wasn't pulled. But I didn't want to have to take away from someone else's time, and from their points, so I'm glad it was me. I can just let you all know this now and then we can move on with the stories and everything next time."

We were silent. This time, I was ready for more of the same and when he started off that way—the same somber and realistic way he started his last story—it made me believe even more that it was just an act. He'd become really good at this, and it made his stories better. He didn't have to have the scariest stories if he was the only one who had true stories to tell. But the problem was, he'd already used this tactic. He got out to a pretty big lead with the 'this is real' strategy, but now he was dipping back into the well one too many times. After this, no one would have much of a doubt that the 'true story' John was telling was nothing more than an act. It would hurt his credibility when it came to the Nightmare Club, and that would affect his score.

"I know you guys won't believe me, but just like before, I'm not kidding. I've got proof this time. Just—just listen to what happened last night, and then I'll show you what I've got. If you don't want to believe me, you don't have to. I won't even take points for tonight if that will help. We can take the night off or whatever, but please just listen to what happened to me."

We stayed silent. I wanted to take him up on his offer but didn't say a word. It seemed like John hoped we would all say no because we were his friends, that we all would want to win fairly. That was true; we all wanted to win, and we knew what was fair and what wasn't. Still, that he'd even offered... It made me believe the sincerity of his story. The only one who might have taken John up on his offer was Chuck, but even he said nothing.

"I was just sleeping in bed the other night, like usual. I-I usually go to bed a little earlier the night before we come out here because I know I'm going to be up late. I don't want to be sitting here super tired or anything. But I've been so tired from football that going to bed early and falling right to sleep is simple. Anyway, I'm off topic. I was sleeping in bed, and I woke up in the middle of the night to piss. It happens sometimes, you know?

"Anyway, I go down the hall to the bathroom and then head back to my room. I lay back down in bed and I hear what sounds like mice or squirrels or something up against my bedroom window. You've all seen my house; you know my bedroom window. It's on that back corner. Animals come by at night sometimes because I'm so low to the ground, but they never pick or pull at the window. They just sort of pass by. This was a different kind of sound. It was there for too long; it didn't sound like an animal at all. I look out and, of course, there's nothing there. Then I look up and happen to catch the moon. It was just that small, thin sliver of a moon, just like the other night."

He looked up at the sky, and there it was, a small fingernail, just like he described.

"I look for another few seconds, don't see anything, and so I just assume it was a big bug that slammed against my screen or something. I turn to lay back down. The sound comes again, though. And I realize it wasn't from outside my window, but from somewhere *inside my room.* So I spin around quick and hit the switch of the light on my nightstand. Guys, he was standing there in my room. Clear as day. Mr. Nightmare. He had that top hat pulled down low so the shadows covered his face again, but the top of his hat nearly hit my ceiling. He was just standing there, *towering* over me. And he didn't say a fucking thing at first. I fell backward, down onto my bed.

"'What the fuck are you doing! Help,' I shouted, hoping my mom or dad would hear me. But they both sleep like fucking rocks and wouldn't hear me all the way upstairs when I'm down in the basement.

"He stood there just looking at me. I assume he was looking at me... I couldn't see his eyes, thank fucking Christ."

As John spoke, I knew Mr. Nightmare was going to talk at some point because John would want to work his Mr. Nightmare-voice into the story. I wasn't buying it, though, and when that voice showed up—the one that had chilled me last time—I'd know for sure he was just making up a new version of the same story. No matter what kind of proof he had. I didn't know I'd hear the voice so soon, though.

"'John?' Mr. Nightmare took a step forward. 'You've done well, and you've certainly fed me some. You've allowed me to keep my strength up. But I need more. I know you can get more nightmares for me. Right?'

"When he stepped forward, I just wanted to bolt out of my room, up the stairs, and right out of the house. But my legs felt locked in place. I didn't realize it, but when he'd moved forward, he locked his hands around both my ankles. I'm pretty strong, but I couldn't move. I tried to push, kick, fight my way out of his grip, but my legs wouldn't budge. The rest of my body thrashed around, but my legs—frozen.

"He leaned forward and down to my level. As he did, the shadow that covered his face started to disappear. Light crept up his chin…further, further, further. Finally, I couldn't take it anymore. I didn't want to see that face again.

"'Stop! Stop,' I said. He knew what I meant and stood back up, the shadow returning to his face.

"'Does this mean you'll help me, John?' he asked in that god-awful voice.

"'What do you need me to do?' I kept my eyes focused on my blankets. I couldn't look up at him. But I got the feeling he was going to show me his face before he left, whether I wanted to see it or not. It was how he made his escape last time. Why would this visit be any different?

"'I need you,' he said from above me, his vice grip grasp making my ankles throb. 'Either get more nightmares out of those friends of yours, or get more kids to join that club. I need more nightmares. You've helped me, but not enough. I need more. I need more. I need more.'

"By the end, he was shouting and squeezing down harder on my ankles, I thought for sure he was going to break them, shatter the bones. But when he finished talking, he threw his head back and looked up at the ceiling. When he did, his hat fell off behind him, and I heard it hit the floor. Then he laughed. This deep evil laugh like nothing I'd ever heard before. I tried again to break away, but I still couldn't move.

"Then he looked back down at me. With his hat gone, there was nothing to keep his face in the shadows. I closed my eyes tight after catching only the slightest glimpse of his face. It didn't knock me out, but I was close. I fucking prayed out loud, shouting, whimpering, crying 'please God, please, please make him go away. Make him stop.'

"My pleading only made Mr. Nightmare laugh harder. I pissed the bed, and then felt bile rise up in my throat, but I managed to choke it down. My room filled with the sound of his hysterical, incessant shrieks. And then, like flipping a switch, my room was silent. The grip on my ankles was gone. I couldn't see and didn't dare look, because the last thing I wanted to see was his face.

"I'm not sure how long I sat there in bed, my legs still frozen in the position he held them in. My eyes clamped shut tight. Somehow tears snuck their way out through them, because I felt the drips on my cheeks. It was only after a few moments, or maybe longer, that I realized I was mumbling to myself, in a half-whisper, half-whine that still makes me embarrassed to think about.

"'Please God, please God, please God, please God,' I kept saying over and over in that tiny little kid voice.

"When I realized I was saying it out loud and not just in my head, I stopped. I held my lips closed tight, same as my eyes.

"I eventually came to the realization that, as much as I didn't want to, I'd have to open my eyes eventually and just hope that he really was gone. I hadn't heard a sound in a while and I couldn't feel Mr. Nightmare there in the room with me anymore. I couldn't hear breathing other than my own or any of the other small noises a person makes when they are standing in one spot for a long time that they don't even notice. The room was silent and I was almost positive it was empty except for me. So I opened my eyes.

"And he was still there.

"'Get to work, young Johnathan!' he said.

"Before I could react, his face— something that was both real and entirely different from anything I'd seen—was right in front of mine. He pulled back just as my brain swirled and scrambled inside my skull. I vomited in my bed, then I fell forward.

"I don't remember my head hitting the bed, but, for a second time, he'd made me pass out. When I came to this morning, the sun was shining in through the windows. I had dried chunks of puke on my face. I peeled myself off the bed, and it reeked of puke and urine. I used a clean part of my sheets to wipe off my face as best I could, then I rolled them up with my piss-soaked shorts and threw the whole thing in the corner of my closet. I washed it all this morning after my parents left for work. Afterward, I hopped in the shower and washed myself off, and tried to get rid of the memories of what happened. But obviously, that didn't work. When I was getting dressed, before I left to meet you guys at The Field, I was putting on my socks and I noticed my ankles were all bruised in the shape of his hands."

With that, John lifted his foot onto the log in the middle of where we all sat. He had his socks pulled up pretty high, but that was normal. He pushed the sock down below the top of his sneaker and there, just at the bony part of his ankle, was a deep purple bruise. Marcus even flipped on his flashlight to get a better look. Once we'd all seen what he wanted us to see, John pulled his sock back up and finished his story.

"The other ankle looks the same, and I-I really don't know what to do, guys. I'm not sure what I should do from here. I'm hoping we can figure this out together. I think, maybe, I've bitten off more than I can chew here. I can't do this alone."

He was done. The fear on his face, the sadness in his voice, was palpable. He was my friend; had been for a long time. I *wanted* to believe him. My body wanted to go to him, to hug him, tell him we would help him. That of course we would all be there for him and help him solve this problem. Was it just some crazy person terrorizing John for some reason? Or was he doing this to other kids that no one knew about it? Those were the questions I held in my heart as we sat in silence. No one knew what to say.

But while I had those questions in my heart, I had others in my head. They were different types of questions, though. Why was he continuing to call on us to help him as part of his story? Did he need to get some real help if he was purposefully bruising himself to get more points in this game? Because that may have just gone a step too far. Were we really supposed to believe these stories?

The debate raged on in my head while John stood in the middle of the circle of fallen logs, his back to the fire, his eyes pleading for help. I looked up at him from my seated position unsure of what to do or say. So I looked away, and avoided eye contact.

Then I stood and moved closer to Chuck, who was standing with Merrie. Marcus came over and joined us, too. We were almost huddling.

John remained by himself, watching us.

Merrie was the first to speak, but in a hushed tone. "What do we do?"

The breeze was light, but it rustled the leaves. I didn't know if John could hear us talking.

"I don't know. But I don't wanna leave here without having some idea of where this goes from here." Marcus said. "If it's really a problem, he wouldn't wait until we were out here in the middle of the night. Right?" He appeared unnerved and angry; it was all over his face.

Chuck nodded. "Yeah. *If* this was real. Like, really a problem he needed our help with. A real person after him… Why the hell would he drag us out here in the middle of the night to ask us for help?"

I didn't say anything. Whatever needed to be said had already been said. I didn't see the need to rehash it.

We each nodded. No one had to tell Chuck that he would be the one to confront John about all this.

Our huddle broke.

"You guys going to vote me out of the group or something now?" John asked.

"John, no. Of course not. You're our friend. We care about you. How long have you and I been doing stuff together? And Anna? Marcus and Merrie, they haven't been around as long, but they care about you, too. They're part of the group now, right?" Chuck waited for a response.

"Yeah. Yeah. I know, Chuckie." John's voice cracked. "It's just been hard, you know?"

"What do you mean, John? Look," Chuck said, "if you say you need help… If this guy—Mr. Nightmare—is really after you, of course we'll help you. But we have questions. *Real* questions. Not Nightmare Club questions."

"What are they?"

Chuck put his arm around John and the two sat on a log together, side by side, arm in arm. Merrie, Marcus, and I stood back and let them talk, though we stayed close so we could hear every word.

"If it's dangerous, John, wouldn't we be better off in our houses at night instead of out here in the woods where no one knows where we are?"

John nodded but didn't answer.

"So, in our heads, it makes us think you're just doing this to earn points. Because we know you wouldn't want to put us in harm's way."

Again, John nodded.

"And if it was real, why would you wait until now to tell us? We were together all day, John. Tell us then. If this is real life shit, tell us during the day so we can have a whole day to figure out what to do about this guy. You know we'll help you, like I said. Either it's real, and you treat it like a real thing. Or it's not, and you tell it like a story here at night, then we move on. But this stuff—asking us to help you when we all still think it's just your competitive ass trying to earn a few more points—doesn't make it easy on us."

John put his face in his hands and cried. It was strange to see this from him. When we were younger, he crashed his bike and skinned his knee pretty good and that got the tears flowing, but we were just little kids then. Second or third grade, if that. That was different. I never expected to see him cry from something like this.

Again, I wanted to go to him. I felt Merrie pull at my arm and saw she wanted to go to him, too. But I held her back.

Marcus put his arms around both of us. "Let him work this out. We've got to know the truth tonight."

"There—there's more," John said through the tears and the sniffling.

"Well, tell us. What else is there?" Chuck said.

"I can't tell it to you."

"Why?"

John said something though heavy tears I couldn't understand. It came out as a high-pitched squeal.

"I couldn't understand that, buddy," Chuck said. He rubbed John's back like a mother consoling a young child.

John took a loud, long breath in and let it out slowly.

"Because he told me if I told you that—that part of the story I leave out every time, the part he reminds me of when he comes—that he'd kill you. He said if I told anyone anything, one of you would die, and it would look like an accident. So, so you know... I won't tell you that part. But please believe me. We need to keep meeting here. We need to keep getting nightmares from each other. So that he stays happy, or—or fed—or whatever it is he does with these nightmares. But we have to keep meeting, okay? I'll change my stories. I'll make them normal, like yours. But we *have* to keep meeting, okay?"

"Okay," Chuck said. He pulled John against him, then gave the three of us a nod. We joined them, surrounded John, and embraced in a hug.

Not long after, we made the silent walk through the woods, into the neighborhood and then home. There were no conversations. No funny jokes or laughing between friends. We just walked home together in silence.

That night, once more, we all dreamed of Mr. Nightmare.

Chapter 8

The change in John started pretty much immediately after that. When we'd walked into the woods that first night, he had been the starting quarterback on the freshmen football team. Within a week he'd dropped to second string. By the end of the season, he was third string. It wasn't just his athletic performance that had changed, either. He'd lost weight and looked physically different, less healthy. He was thin, his eyes sunk deeper into his skull, dark circles around them. His cheeks were gaunt, making his already prominent cheekbones more visible. According to Chuck, John's grades were also slipping.

While he was never going to get straight As like Chuck, John always managed mostly Bs with a few Cs mixed in like he did in the first quarter of school that year. After that, his grades plummeted. Chuck told me the second term saw him fail most of his classes with a few Ds from teachers who probably felt bad for him and were trying to help him out.

When adults started to notice the changes in John, the first people they came to were Chuck and I. The phone rang one night, and Mom answered. It was John's mom. They talked for a while.

Later that night, when I was getting ready for bed, I heard Dad go into Chuck's room and talk to him. Mom came into my room right after, and we talked, too. She asked about John; if he was acting different or getting into drugs or alcohol. I told her no, because that was the truth. In spite of school, we spent a lot of time together still, and if anyone knew whether John was doing drugs or anything like that, it would have been Chuck, Merrie, Marcus, and me. And he wasn't.

But for all of the physical problems he appeared to be having, and whatever mental issues that might have gone along with them, his personality didn't change all that much. He was still the same friend I always knew. He joked about the same things and talked about the same things. He came up with ideas for games on weekends when we were able to go to The Field—which was less and less as the weather got colder. But we all saw each other regularly.

And we still had the meetings. Every weekend in November we met. In December, we met too; even the bitter cold nights. We found extra wood around The Dwelling to build a bigger fire on those nights, instead of sitting on the logs, we stood around the metal barrel fire warming us while we told stories.

True to his word, John didn't talk about Mr. Nightmare, outside or at the meetings. As far as we knew, Mr. Nightmare was gone. But still, John led in the scoring week after week. When he told those stories, he became a different person. He could change his voice to match whatever ghost or monster he wanted to sound like. He pretended to be sad or angry or scared and could show those emotions at the drop of a hat. But he never mentioned Mr. Nightmare. The few times we tried to bring it up outside of our meetings, he just shook his head, made a joke, and moved on. After a while, we stopped trying.

It was the middle of March before the subject came up again.

John's grades were still low, but they had leveled off and he was trying hard enough in school third quarter to keep from failing—though he still had Ds across the board, according to Chuck. I suspected it was that baseball season was during the fourth quarter, and he wouldn't be allowed to play if he was failing too many classes. John was the best pitcher most people in town had ever seen. When he entered the high school as a freshman, it was already well-known throughout school that he would be a starting pitcher on the varsity team later that spring. His weight loss and poor performance at the end of the football season did nothing to change that.

It was a few days before the start of the spring sports season and John, Merrie, Chuck, and I were at

The Field. It was the first really warm day of spring. It had been a while since it had rained or snowed, so the fields were dry and the ground solid. John had his bucket of baseballs and was throwing them against the concrete back of the dugout. We all stood around watching him.

"I don't have to do it," John said as he picked up another ball and whipped it against the back of the dugout. "I could wait until practice starts, but it helps loosen my arm up. The more stretched out I am on the first day of practice, the better it'll be. I have to compete with all those older kids for a spot, so, you know, if I can throw a little harder than all of them the first week, the coaches will notice that."

"I get it," Merrie said. "But why not just play catch. We're all here. We all have gloves; we could just play catch."

John laughed. "Sorry. I don't mean to laugh. But I can get way more throws in doing it this way than playing catch. Plus, no offense, but I throw pretty hard and those gloves wouldn't protect your hands very much."

He threw the ball at the dugout; it sizzled as it left his hand.

"You'd need to have a catcher's mitt. For real." He picked up another ball and threw it against the dugout again. It bounced back towards us, but fell well short of hitting any of us.

"Your arm seems strong, John. Remember at the end of football season when you felt like your arm was getting tired? Was that just because the ball was heavier? Too much throwing?" Chuck wasn't pressing for information; he was just curious.

We'd long since stopped asking John about his new physical appearance or grades. He was the same to us so we treated him the same. It was just a normal question, but Chuck didn't get an expected answer.

"Nah. That was more because I wasn't sleeping or eating." The words tumbled out of John's mouth like it wasn't a big deal. He bent down to grab a ball off the ground and then stopped. He let out a sigh and muttered the word "shit" under his breath.

Merrie, Chuck, and I shared a look.

"What do you mean?" I asked, my hand on John's back.

"Fuck. I didn't mean to say that. Can't we just pretend I didn't say that?"

"No, come on. It's okay; you can tell us. It's all good," Chuck said.

John ran his hand through his dirty blond hair that I only now noticed was a little bit longer than he usually let it grow. His lips tightened, and he stood up and put his hands on his hips. In his eyes was a look I hadn't seen since the nights he talked about Mr. Nightmare. It had been a while, but the look was haunting. I'd never forget seeing his face that way.

"So let's get Marcus and go find a place to talk. No waiting for the meeting this time. I'll do it the way we talked about. But you guys asked, okay? I was content not saying anything. Remember that."

"Why don't you guys stay here and I'll run and see if Marcus is home. We can just talk here. Does that sound good?" Chuck said.

"Yeah. That works," John said.

He began scooping up baseballs again. I thought he was going to keep throwing, like a way to keep his mind off of it, but he just tossed the balls back in the bucket.

I started helping him, and then Merrie did, too. But he stopped us.

"No. Please don't, guys," he said. "Let me. It gives my mind something to do. I'm sorry about this. More sorry I said that. Shit. I thought it was all behind us. You know, Anna-banana? I messed up this fall, and I've been working my ass off to keep things good. Keep things moving forward. My grades were terrible. I lost all that weight. Stopped sleeping. But I've been turning it around lately. You know?"

"We know. Come on, let's just get these balls picked up and then we can go sit in the dugout. You don't want to get too far along with this until Chuck and Marcus get here, right?"

"Yeah, yeah. You're right. Thanks, both of you. I don't know what I'd do without you guys. For real."

We didn't reply.

I leaned against the dugout while John finished collecting the baseballs, then the three of us went and sat in the dugout and waited. It felt like a long time, but it probably wasn't. I wanted to say something. The truth was, over the winter I'd developed something of a crush on John. When we were younger, in fourth or fifth grade, I thought I liked him because he was the only boy I knew well who wasn't my brother. But as we aged, I realized it was more of a friendship than me actually liking him.

But over the summer we had started the Nightmare Club, and as fall and then winter came, my feelings for him changed. He was still my friend, but I noticed things about him I hadn't always seen. He was becoming more important to me; it was more than just a friendship in my head. I didn't really understand the whole situation and how I was feeling until I found out he had asked a girl in his grade to the freshman class spring formal dance in May. Obviously, he would want to go with a girl who was a freshman, and not an eighth grader, but I was hurt by it nonetheless. My jealousy in that moment told me for sure that my feelings were changing.

I could never tell anyone about that, of course. Not Chuck, not John. Not even Merrie, who was the only girl I considered a friend. The idea of the information getting back to John or even Chuck was enough for me to keep my mouth shut. I was young enough that if something were to ever happened between John and me, there was time to let it happen on its own. I didn't have to force it.

The sun dropped lower and reached into the dugout where we sat. It shone in our eyes through the fencing. I put a hand up to block it.

Then we heard Chuck's voice.

"Hey. Where are you guys? I got Marcus."

John jumped up and walked to the end of the dugout and stuck his head around the side. "In here."

Chuck and Marcus came around the side and then sat down with us in the dugout.

"Okay. We're all here." Chuck said.

"I know. I know…" John took a deep breath. "Just give me a minute."

Merrie slid next to me on the bench so our legs touched. Chuck sat next to her, and Marcus next to him. There was just enough room in the dugout for John to stand in front of us, his back pressed against the chain link fence.

"This isn't story time," he said. "We're not in the woods, and it's not night. I didn't even want to ever tell you guys about all this, honest."

"We believe you," Marcus said. "I think we're past all of that. This is just friend stuff, not Nightmare Club stuff. We're here for you."

"Okay, so. You know, after that last time we talked about Mr. Nightmare, remember I said there were other parts of the conversation he told me I couldn't tell you?"

Silence, but we all nodded our understanding. No one could forget that night. Not in six months, or six years, or sixty years.

"Okay. Right. Yeah. Of course, you do. So, you know, he— well, he kept visiting me for a while after that. Always at night. But he never said anything or did anything. He was just sort of…there. A lot. Not all the time, but I'd wake up and I could see him in the corner of my room, just his shadow, standing there so tall and with that top hat. It's hard to mistake him for anything else."

"He didn't do anything to you, or say anything?" I asked.

John shook his head. "No, nothing. Just there, is all. Like he wanted to me know that he was still around. Still watching us, or watching me. You know, reminding me about everything."

"Okay," Chuck said. "And then what happened?"

"Well, nothing else happened really. Not with him, anyway. He was just there so much, I got paranoid. I stopped sleeping. The first night I decided to stay awake as long as I could. Eventually, I passed out in bed. When I woke up, he was there again. That happened a few nights in a row, so I realized I couldn't lay down in bed, because if I did, I'd fall asleep sooner or later and he would be there.

"So, I stopped getting in bed. I'd say good night to my parents and go down to my room. I'd do jumping jacks or push-ups or sit ups and just pace back and forth to keep the blood flowing so I wouldn't fall sleep. That worked pretty well, but as soon as I stopped moving, my eyes would droop closed and that was all he needed. Suddenly he was there and I'd have stayed awake for no reason. Then it got to the point where, even if I wanted to, I couldn't, because I knew he would be there the next time I opened my eyes.

"It was around the same time I stopped eating. Not sure if I have an explanation for that, but it was probably because I was sleeping less and not taking care of myself, and I just wasn't hungry. I had a hard time concentrating in school because of it, too. Which explains my grades. But I didn't want to put all this on you guys, because I knew you'd try to help me. So I pretended everything was fine, and its why you didn't really notice a change. I was tired, but still the same guy."

"They asked us if you were hanging out with new kids or on drugs," I said, remembering that night in my room with Mom.

"Yeah, your parents wanted to check with us, so Dad came to talk to me and Mom talked to Anna," Chuck added.

"Everyone asked me the same stuff, too." John ran his hand through his hair again. "Teachers, guidance counselors, the nurse, coaches, parents. They all assumed I was getting into drugs or something. What was I supposed to tell them? That some guy was just appearing in my room and watching me sleep every night? He's got a scary face and might be magical. That would just ensure them I was on drugs."

"John," Merrie said. I felt her tense next to me. I had a feeling she didn't really want to hear the answer to the question she was about to ask. "What do *you* think he is? A person? A ghost? Something—I don't know—something else?"

John laughed. "You know, I've been asking myself that question for the last six months. I have no idea. He held my legs down, and that felt pretty real to me."

We went on like that for a while, volleying questions back and forth. John always gave us some form of the same answers, over and over. He rehashed the same stories he'd told us in the woods, but with less detail. He also told us he didn't know to a bunch of questions, and it was hard to read what everyone was thinking. I never really believed everything he was saying was true. Not the first time he told the stories, and not that day in the dugout. There was something about the way he told the story that, while convincing, also made me think he was making it up, or leaving something out.

Of course, he had an excuse for that too, because he told us there was something about his meetings with Mr. Nightmare that he couldn't tell us.

If he did tell us, Mr. Nightmare would kill one of us and make it look like an accident. Every reason we had to doubt him, he had an explanation for, it seemed.

He was our best friend; we should have believed him. *I* should have believed him. But for some reason, I still felt like he wasn't telling us the truth. And I felt horrible for it.

Chapter 9

A few days after our meeting in the dugout, spring sports started at the high school. It meant that, after school, Merrie and I were on our own. Marcus and Chuck had made the junior varsity baseball team and John, of course, was on the varsity team. Both teams practiced every day like they had during the fall and winter. We didn't mind the time to ourselves, though. I had softball starting in a few weeks, but that was only a few days a week. Merrie took dance three days a week starting after our spring break. When we could get together, we would.

Come spring, we didn't always go to The Field after our homework was done because there were usually little kids baseball practices there. It was always too crowded for us to find a spot to ourselves. But after school one day, I left home and walked toward Merrie's house. I knocked on her door, and her mom answered.

"Oh, hi, Anna. How are you? I think Merrie is done her homework. Let me go check for you. Do you want to come in?"

"No, I'm okay." I shook my head. "It's nice out. I'll just sit out here until she's done."

I sat on the top step by their front door. Even though it was in the same neighborhood as ours, their house was bigger than ours. Both of Merrie's parents worked, and they probably made more money together than my dad ever could. Mom didn't work, and though I never felt like we missed out on things, I wondered what it was like to live in a bigger house with more space. To be able to get everything you wanted for your birthday.

Every year, my parents asked us what we wanted. We always had to choose carefully. If there were two inexpensive things, we might get them. If we asked for two presents, we typically only got one. It was in our best interest to figure out the one thing we wanted for our birthday and give that as the answer. That way we made sure we got it. I always wondered what it would be like to ask for two or even three things for your birthday and get both of them every year. Merrie and her sister probably got more than one birthday present if they asked for it.

"Hey." I heard Merrie's voice from behind.

"Hey, that was quick."

"Yeah." Merrie pulled the door shut behind her and then let the screen door slam shut. "I was almost done my math homework, but it was killing me. So I just said screw it, because I could get the rest done tomorrow before class started."

"Nice. I usually leave a few questions of homework for before class, too. The field is probably packed with kids right now. Where do you wanna go?"

"Well, let's swing by the field. I have an idea." Merrie raised her eyebrows and gave a smirk that told me whatever she had in mind, it wasn't something we were supposed to do.

The main roads in Whitmon were all set up in straight lines. It wasn't hard to figure out where you were headed because every major road ran straight north and south or east and west. If you wanted to go north, all you had to do was find a main road and eventually you would get there. If you wanted to go west, same thing. It was easy to get around that way.

But once you got into the neighborhoods, the idea of straight lines disappeared. The roads weaved and zigged and zagged and curled back on themselves in a way that made no sense. There were cul-de-sacs everywhere, and it was normal to see a car pull onto a street in our neighborhood, turn around to leave, and then come back five minutes later because they had no idea where they were headed. They'd eventually pull over and ask for directions or pull out a map, if they had one.

We had two advantages when we moved from one place to another inside our neighborhood. First, we

knew all the roads. We knew the long ones that turned
and twisted. We knew the small ones that connected
the dead-end roads together. We knew the ones that
weren't even on the map and consisted only of a small
dirt road connecting two longer roads. Second, we
knew which yards we could cut through to get where
we were going. When we were all together, we
knew—or our parents did—most of the people in the
neighborhood and were friends with them all. So, if we
wanted to cut through a yard to get somewhere faster,
chances were, it was okay for us to do that. So, we
took full advantage.

Instead of taking the long way up and around to
the field on the other side of the neighborhood, Merrie
and I cut through no less than six backyards. We took a
quick detour through the elementary school parking lot
and cut a good ten minutes off of our walking time.
Merrie didn't mention what she had planned if the field
was full. When we saw the parking lot full of cars and
kids with baseball gloves and bats running in every
direction, we shared a look

Both of us shook our heads.

"No way," we both said at nearly the same
time.

I laughed, then said, "So what was this other
idea you had?"

"Well, what if we went to The Dwelling during
the day? I've never seen it in the daylight. Might be
interesting."

My eyes widened. I'd never even thought of the fact that none of us—except John—

had ever seen the place in the daytime. Unless Chuck or Marcus made a trip and didn't tell anyone, which seemed unlikely.

"You know what? That sounds really awesome, actually. Let's do it."

"Yes!" Merrie held her hand up, and I slapped her five.

It was a childish thing to do, but at the time it felt like the only way to get out my emotions. We were going to have our own adventure. We'd be able to tell Chuck and John and Marcus that we saw The Dwelling during the day. I wondered what it looked like.

Using the same strategy we'd used to get to the field, we cut through yards and along little mostly unused roads to get to the end of Red Bird Drive. Even the street looked different in the daytime. At night, the streetlights would cast a pallor of evenly spaced circles down the road. When we walked down the road at night, it was as if the darkness was only a step or two behind us, waiting for us to turn our backs to it and stop paying attention so it could reach out and envelop us. Over the weeks of going up and down this road, it had become normal to feel that creeping darkness. So much so that I didn't really notice it anymore.

This trip was altogether different. It was late afternoon, so the sun was low in the sky, but it was still light. Everything glowed with the sun behind us and our shadows stretched out in front. It would be dark before long and—though we weren't afraid of getting lost or being in the woods after dark—we didn't have a flashlight or any of the guys to protect us. It would have to be a quick trip.

We reached the end of Red Bird Drive and stopped in pretty much the same spot Chuck, John, and I had the very first time we made the walk.

"Even the street looks different in the daytime. I don't come down here really, ever," Merrie said.

"I know. Me too. Let's do it."

We stepped into the woods and made our way through the trees. The first thing I noticed were the colors. At night, everything was dark, gray, lifeless. In the daylight, the new buds on the trees were still the light shade of green that blankets most of the trees in our area in the spring. And those greens surrounded us, reaching out over our heads and closing around behind us as we passed the tree line.

Beyond that were some pine trees featuring the darker greens as well as some low shrubs. Leaves covered the ground, but I was surprised that—nearly six months since they'd changed color and fallen from the trees above—they still held most of the color that made them beautiful in the fall.

We trudged through the leaves, but I noticed the makings of a path beneath them. I realized it was probably made by the Nightmare Club repeatedly returning here. I smiled at that. If we continued meeting with the same frequency, the path would become more prominent and might be something that would last years after we stopped using it.

I spotted a tall V-shaped tree we often used as a landmark. From there, I veered right, with Merrie close behind me. Within a minute, we were at The Dwelling.

The barrel, halfway filled with black, charred wood, was blue. I knew because I'd seen it under the light of the flashlight before. In my head, it had always been a dingy, dark gray, and covered in rust. But now the blue was bright and vibrant. Around us were bushes with dark red buds on them, not the green ones I'd been expecting. The earth was packed beneath our feet. It was clear the area was being used. Maybe just by us, but I never forgot what Chuck had told me about older kids using an area like this to drink without getting in trouble.

"This is crazy," Merrie said. "It's like a whole new place."

"Yeah," I said, standing in the middle with my back to the barrel, looking around at surroundings simultaneously familiar and unfamiliar.

"Hey, Anna. Can I ask you something?"

"Yeah, of course."

Merrie sat down on the end of one of the logs, which had become her unofficial spot. We'd all kind of picked our own spots each time we came. It was unspoken, of course, but each week we all sat in the same place. That was Merrie's spot.

Humans are creatures of habit.

"What's going on?" I said, and sat down next to her.

"It's been a while since we talked about it, but then, when it all came up again the other day, I can't get my mind off of it."

"Mr. Nightmare?" I sighed.

"Yeah, I don't know what's real, what's not real. It's just hard for me. I want to believe John—I know you do, too—but the way everything went down, just the nature of this Mr. Nightmare guy in general, if it is real, it's gotta be like a demon or a ghost or something. If he isn't real—which I'm sad to say is more likely—then I'm afraid John is losing his mind. I just don't know what to think."

"I know. Chuck and I have talked about it a lot these last few days. We came to the same conclusion. Most likely it's just in his head. Or maybe there *was* some guy here once, and seeing him just messed with John's head or something. I don't know. But yeah, I'm worried about him for sure, because I think—"

We both looked around at the sound of leaves rustling and twigs snapping behind us. The sound came from the same direction from which we'd arrived. My first thought was that someone had followed us. But I stood up, my eyes wide—so did Merrie's—and we saw an impossibly tall man wearing a top hat come sliding through the woods toward us.

"Run," I whispered, but neither of us moved.

"Hello." His voice rang out from every direction. It was much worse than John had made it seem—low and scratchy, but strong and frightening at the same time.

My stomach clenched and tied itself in a knot. I wanted to puke. But I couldn't tear my eyes from him.

"Come on. Let's go," Merrie said.

She groped for my hand and found it. We turned and both slammed into the barrel we'd forgotten was right behind us, standing like a sentinel watching over The Dwelling. It was starting to feel less and less like this place belonged to us.

The impact with the barrel knocked us down in the dirt. We scrambled to our feet, but he was there, standing over us. I looked up at him. The low sun behind him created a silhouette so we couldn't see his face, which had become legend among our little group. Instead, we only saw the tall, lanky body, those long arms, and the top hat sitting just slightly off to one side.

"You run and you die." His voice made me want to scream.

The knot returned in my stomach; my breath was out of control. I felt like I was going to pass out. Merrie was next to me, her hand tight around mine. I gave her a look and didn't see any of the stress or worry on her face that coursed through my veins. She was angry, determined, and ready to fight this guy if it came down to it. She was anything but afraid.

"Who are you?" Merrie asked, her voice strong and loud.

"I think you know my name, Merrie. Just like I know both of yours. Isn't that right, Anna?" He laughed. It was the only sound worse than his voice.

I felt my hands move toward my ears, but Merrie gripped me tight and held my hand in place. She was staying strong. She was keeping us both strong.

"Oh right, Mr. Nightmare. I get it. So, was it your dad who had the last name Nightmare? No, it was probably your mom, because you're definitely a fucking bastard."

Mr. Nightmare took a step back, as if he wasn't expecting this kind of fight from Merrie. Neither did I, to be honest. I'd never heard anything like that from her before. She wasn't going to back down.

"Well, at least now I know who the little bitch of the Nightmare Club is. I'm not going to lie to you, I was under the assumption that it would be Anna-banana here." He lifted a long, bony finger and pointed it at me.

"I—" I stammered at the sound of the name only John ever used.

"You don't get to call her that. Now, we came out to see what this place looked like in the light. I have no idea why you're here. So talk, or we'll leave."

Mr. Nightmare laughed again and stepped closer to us. He was on the other side of the log we'd been sitting on. I kept my eyes focused on his chest. I searched myself for the courage to do what Merrie was, but couldn't find it. Chuck was the smart one. I was the planner. John was the creative one. Marcus, the responsible one. Maybe Merrie was the tough one.

"Since you don't seem like you want to make small talk, little bitch, I'll skip right to the point. I *am* real, and I *can* feed off your nightmares. Your friend John loves you and wants to keep you alive. That's why he keeps most of what I say to him a secret. He knows if he tells too much, you'll all die."

He stepped over the log toward us, his feet only a few inches from ours now. I kept my eyes averted from his face. Even Merrie's tough exterior had begun to crack. Her lip quivered for a brief moment as she did her best to avoid looking right at his face.

"I don't need to rip your heads off or tear your stomach open and leave your guts and entrails all over the woods to kill you, either. Although I might like to see that." He reached out and almost ran a spindly, knotty finger against Merrie's cheek. His skin wasn't just pale, but white as paper. "No, no. If he tells anyone the things we have talked about then one of you must die. At your funeral, everyone will say 'oh, what a terrible accident' or 'she wasn't really like that. I don't know what came over her.' No one will ever know it was me, because that's the way I work.

"And when you die, your parents, grandparents, brother or sisters—anyone who knew you—will all have dreams. Bad dreams. *Nightmares.* And when they do, I get stronger. And if you're scared now—I knew Anna was the moment she first saw me, and even you Merrie, a tough little bitch, is scared now that I am so close—you wouldn't want to see me after I've had the nightmares of adults. Those are the best kind of nightmares. They are harder to get, but the best kind."

He put his arms out to either side and took another step forward, almost right on top of us. Even if we wanted to, we couldn't run. He'd managed to freeze us in place long enough to prevent that.

"Wh-what do you want with us?" I managed to get out, my voice shaking. I was trying my best to sound as strong as Merrie.

"Ah, she *does* speak. Little Anna-banana, who has a crush on John Workman. Who dreams of him in her sleep. And not just the nightmares I get to feed on. No, no, no no. The dreams she has of John Workman are those *other* kinds of dreams. The dreams you never want to tell anyone about—even your best friend. Yes, Merrie, she dreams about John. Not every night. Most nights her dreams are just regular boring dreams about what happened that day. But sometimes she dreams about my friend John, and sometimes she has nightmares about him. And sometimes, she dreams about me. Picture that. Me, the man of your dreams."

My face burned. I refused to give his words any credence by looking over at Merrie. I kept my eyes locked straight ahead. Then he broke out into a horrible, deafening laugh. It surrounded us, much as his words had earlier. His laugh didn't emanate just from his mouth; it came from everywhere. And it held us in place as much as his arms blocked our escape.

Then, his arms seemed to stretch even wider, encircling the barrel and trapping us between it and him. I couldn't see his hands anymore; they'd disappeared somewhere behind us. Sitting, we only came up to his waist, so it was easy to keep our eyes off of his face. But I never forgot what John said about seeing it. John had tried not to look, but when Mr. Nightmare finally left him alone, the last thing John saw was his face. Somehow, I knew, when Mr. Nightmare decided to leave now, he'd make sure we both got a good look as well.

"You still didn't tell us what you want," Merrie said. Her voice shook this time. She still sounded strong, but it was clear fear had crept in.

"I just wanted to come for a visit. I know some of the members of your little group don't think I'm real. Before today, I don't think any of you thought I was real. Hell, John only believes in me part of the time, and we've spent so many nights up late talking and sharing stories about our hopes and dreams for the future. But now the two of you have seen me. You know I'm real. So, I'll tell you the same thing I told John, because he seems to have a hard time following directions. I don't want to have to kill any members of your club, because I have plans for all of you, if you can manage to continue to meet. That's what I need from you. John knows this has to continue. If the Nightmare Club ends, your lives end, too. There is nothing you can do to change that. Even if the two of you think you're strong and want to stand up to me, you can't. You don't even matter to me. Only your dreams matter. So, you two and John will make sure the Nightmare Club continues."

His arms wavered slightly, and the sky darkened. It wouldn't be long before it was nighttime. The last thing I wanted was to be out here in the dark with this guy running around. This needed to end, so I just let him talk, hoping he would leave. I hoped Merrie was thinking the same thing.

"But more importantly, you will never talk about me to the other members of your club. You won't even talk about me to each other. After today, the two of you won't talk about what went on here this afternoon. You will *never* mention this again. And if John tries to bring up the subject of Mr. Nightmare, you *must* stop him or someone *will* die."

We jumped at that.

"Do you understand?" he asked.

We nodded.

"Good. If you decide to tell a pretend story like my friend John did, one of your friends will die. If you just come out and tell them what happened here today, one or more of your friends will die. But if you keep going on like nothing is wrong, and you keep meeting out here in the woods once a week, and giving each other nightmares… Then you may never see or hear from me again. Which of those two choices, my little ladies, would you like to move forward with?"

At first, my brain didn't realize he was asking us a question, I'd fallen into a trance listening to him talk. Figuring out what he was saying, then wondering if he'd also met up with Chuck and Marcus at some point, making us all promise not to tell the others about him.

"I'm waiting." He bent down, bringing his face closer to ours. It was a threat.

"We won't say anything to anyone. Right, Anna?" Merrie turned to look at me.

I returned the look and nodded. "Yep, we won't say anything. Promise."

"Great, then we have nothing to worry about." He leaned closer.

I knew what was coming, but wasn't sure if Merrie did until she shouted at me.

"Close your eyes!"

I did. Something opened them for me.

In that moment, I understand why John refused to say anything about Mr. Nightmare's face. And I-I can't give any details, either. It was—it was terrifying, but awe inspiring at the same time. It was like nothing I'd ever seen. My brain couldn't process it all. That was the only explanation I had for something like this, that affected me this way.

Next to me, I felt Merrie tense. Her hand clawed at mine, but she went rigid and then shrieked. I felt her falling backward toward the barrel behind us and would have tried to stop her descent if it wasn't for the effect his face was having on my own body. Instead of slamming my eyes shut after I got the first glimpse, the grotesquerie of his face held my eyes open, forcing me to stare, no ability to pull myself away. The warmth that spread over the bottom half of my body—I'd find out later—was my bladder emptying. My physical reaction to his face was different than Merrie's, though. My leg muscles loosened, and I crumpled to the ground. The last thing I remembered seeing was the dirt, the leaves, and then Mr. Nightmare's black shoes as he walked away.

Chapter 10

When we woke, it was nearly dark. My crotch and legs were cool from the dampness of my urine and the sunless spring air. Merrie sat with her back against the barrel, rubbing her head. I crawled to her, my muscles still working to find strength. I collapsed next to her and slumped against the barrel.

"Anna…" Merrie's eyes were wet, but tears had yet to appear on her cheeks. Her mouth gave her fear and sadness away. "Was that real?"

"I think it was." I gave a half nod, afraid to say much more. But then the words came spilling out before I could stop them. "But you were so great, so strong, Merrie. I—"

"Stop." She reached out and cupped her hand over my mouth.

My eyes widened.

"We can't talk about it, Anna. Thanks, but we can't say anymore. We just have to—have to go on like it didn't happen."

She was right and I knew it. I nodded, but wanted to share everything with her, what I was feeling and thinking. We had to figure out what we were going to do. We couldn't just let this guy—this monster—hold us hostage, could we? He was trying to force us to remain quiet about what we'd seen. We had no way of knowing if he could follow through with his threat. Could he really kill any, or all, of us and make it look like an accident each time? I wasn't totally buying that, but I also wasn't willing to bet anyone's life on a belief. The safest bet was to remain quiet and see what happened.

If one thing good came out of that afternoon, it was that I no longer questioned John and the stories he'd told us about Mr. Nightmare. Everything had been the truth, as much as he was allowed to tell us. He obviously *wanted* to tell us more, but remained silent because of threats from Mr. Nightmare.

I stood up and put my hand on the barrel, then leaned over to help Merrie up. "Come on. Let's go home. We're strong enough to handle this." I pulled her up

She brushed herself off and pointed at my damp pants. "When you get home, just roll those up in a ball and toss them outside your window. You can bring them to my house tomorrow morning. My parents are both working, so I can wash and dry them and get them back to you. No one will see them, will they?"

"No. That should work."

"Yeah, okay. I'll have some time by myself at home to wash and dry them. Then you can just get them back clean."

"Okay. Thanks, Merrie. It's not too late for you to get home, is it?"

"No, but if they ask I'll just tell them we were down at The Field playing and lost track of time."

"Thanks for everything, Merrie. I'm glad you were here with me this afternoon."

"Thanks. I'm glad you were here, too. If I'm going through anything hard, I know it will be better if you're there with me. And I'm always here for you."

We hugged. I did my best to keep my wet pants away from Merrie.

We left The Dwelling and walked in silence until we reached the corner of Marshall Circle and George Lane. There, we parted ways with a simple, short goodbye and headed to our homes.

The lights were on in the kitchen and I could see the TV illuminating the living room through the front window. It meant Mom was in the kitchen cooking, and Dad was watching TV. It also meant I had a small window to sneak in without either of them seeing my pants. I didn't care if they asked me why I was late getting home. I'd dealt with that a few times and could get out of it, especially if I had an alibi. But if either of them saw my pants, there would be obvious questions. It was better to just not deal with it.

I walked up my driveway casually, staying out of the areas where the light from inside spilled out. As I approached the front door, I slowed my gait and softened each step. I climbed onto the porch and pulled the front door open slowly, silently. As soon as it was open, I heard the sound of the TV. Thank God Dad watched the TV with the volume so loud.

I slipped in through the front door without pulling it closed behind me. Because as soon as I changed, the plan was to sneak back out and pretend like I was just getting home. I walked as softly as I could past the living room, and down the hall to my bedroom, doing my best to avoid putting pressure on any of the squeaky spots on the floor. I shut my door silently and finally exhaled.

After peeling off my wet clothes and changing into dry ones—though my legs still felt sticky with dried urine. I slipped back out of my room and to the front door. This time I whipped the door open a little harder than I usually would have and feigned being out of breath.

"Hey," I gasped, making my announcement to no one in particular. "Sorry I'm late. Merrie and I just lost track of time down at The Field." I kicked off my shoes.

Dad turned his head half way around and gave a wave. "Hey, Anna. It's okay. Dinner's not ready for a few minutes."

The first obstacle was down, but Mom would be a bit harder to convince. She wouldn't just listen to what I said; she would have questions. She always did. Normally, I'd get annoyed. It wasn't as if something bad would have happened to me in those extra ten minutes—usually.

The entire act of sneaking in and covering my tracks had been a welcome distraction. I had to pay attention to what I was doing, and that kept my mind free from thinking about what had happened in the woods. Maybe my brain was protecting me—from thinking about Mr. Nightmare's face—but I was so preoccupied with getting into the house unnoticed and explaining why I was late that I didn't have time to think about Mr. Nightmare or anything that had happened. I was fully—thankfully—in the present.

I might have just gone into my room and hidden until Mom called me for dinner, avoiding the conversation as long as possible. But then we'd be talking over dinner and I'd rather just get the conversation out of the way now, when it was just the two of us, than having it out in front of Chuck and Dad.

"Hey Mom," I said, still huffing a little so she knew I'd run home, trying to get here on time.

"Little bit late, huh?" Mom had her hands on her hips, dish towel in her hand. She looked down her nose at me like she always did when she was curious. Most people would have assumed the look was anger, but I knew better. She just wanted to hear the story. If she believed it, she'd be okay with it. If not, *then* she'd get angry.

It was my time to shine.

"Yeah, I know. I was with Merrie down at The Field. We just lost track of time. You know, Chuck always has his watch on, but he wasn't with us today, obviously, so we didn't realize what time it was until we saw it getting dark. On our way out we asked someone what time it was and that's when we started running." I was still gasping a little, trying my best to talk fast, like I'd just sprinted home.

Mom nodded, a good sign.

"It's hard with the time change, I imagine. Don't worry. I understand." She turned and grabbed a spoon, stirring something in a pot on the stove. From the smell, I'd say it was green beans in her famous garlic sauce. "It's okay this time. But we got you a watch last year for Christmas, right?"

"Yes. I know."

"Just try to remember to wear it and then you won't lose track of time no matter where you are. Deal?"

"Okay," her back was still turned, and I felt the beginnings of a smile form on my lips. I'd done it, without even a call to Merrie's parents to make sure our stories matched. I only hoped Merrie's talk with her parents went as smooth.

"Now, help set the table for dinner. Chuck should be home from practice soon."

I put all the dishes out for dinner. I never really minded helping out around the house. But now that I'd snuck in, changed clothes, and gotten out of being in trouble for coming home late, I no longer had anything to occupy my mind.

My thoughts returned to the woods and Mr. Nightmare. I replayed the whole afternoon in my head. I reviewed how Merrie and I ended up in the woods and whether there was anything I could have done to change it. I didn't think there was. As I reviewed the conversation with Mr. Nightmare in my head, the fear returned. I could almost feel the warm urine that had made my pants wet as I stared up at—at his face.

I almost cried as I set out the forks and knives on the table and thought about the fact I could never talk about this, or my feelings, with anyone. My hands shook so badly, I had to quickly set down the rest of the silverware and take a seat at my spot at the table to hide my nerves.

Behind all of that, making a bad day even worse was the fact that Merrie now knew what I'd been thinking about John. It was possible she just thought Mr. Nightmare was making all of that stuff up about John to scare us, to make us uncomfortable, but I'd never be able to talk about it with her. I'd done such a good job of keeping it hidden and wasn't ready to let anyone know—including Merrie. I would have preferred no one know, ever, but that choice had been taken away from me.

My thoughts started to cycle. I kept thinking the same thing again and again, part of me hoping that by doing this, something would change. But each time I went through the events of that afternoon, it came out the same.

I had to find something to distract myself. I had to figure out a way to tell Chuck what had happened. If he could guess it somehow, it wouldn't be telling him. And if he knew, together we'd find a solution to the problem of Mr. Nightmare.

Chuck came home not long after and we sat as family—like always—and ate. We usually talked about current events or things going on at school. Sometimes we got to hear stories about Dad's work, which we were interested in. There was always something to talk about. That night, though, I didn't say much. I spoke if someone asked me a question, but I didn't just spontaneously join in the conversation.

When we finished eating, Chuck and I cleared the table, and Mom and Dad got to work on the dishes. After that, I went outside and sat on the back porch. Our backyard didn't have a fence like most of our neighbors, but there was enough space between our house and the houses on either side of us that when you sat out there after the sun went down, you felt almost as if you were alone in the world. Darkness moved in around you and, when the kitchen lights were off, it was only the very dim lights from the neighboring houses or the occasional passing car that infringed upon the blanket of darkness that held you close to its heart.

The back door to the house squeaked when it opened. I was so lost in thought that I jumped at the sound of it. I turned, expecting to see Mom standing there, but it was Chuck.

"Hey," he said, and sat down on the porch step next to me.

I slid over a little to my right giving him some room. "Hey."

We sat in silence.

I had the beginnings of a hundred different sentences on the tip of my tongue. I kept coming up with new ways to attack the problem of not being able to tell Chuck what I wanted to. What I *needed* to tell him. But each time I thought about starting in, I pictured him—or Marcus, or John, or Merrie—dead by some freak accident. I saw their funerals and their parents crying. I was crying to myself because I'd known that it was my fault. I could even envision a scenario where I took my own life instead of living with the fact that I was the reason my friend had died. I didn't want that, so I kept my mouth shut.

"What's up with you tonight?" Chuck asked.

"Huh?" I only heard half of his question at first. But it was enough for him to realize something was wrong.

"I can tell when something's wrong with you, Anna. Even if Mom and Dad can't. Just like I can't hide stuff from you for a very long time."

"It's nothing. How was practice?" I knew the change of subject wouldn't get him to drop it, but getting my mind off Mr. Nightmare for minute while he talked about baseball would be a welcomed distraction.

"Oh, it was good. Fine. I'll never be the best player on the team—not like John or anything—but I'm good enough to make the team and play. It's really about enjoying yourself. I don't know. That kinda makes me sound like a loser, right?"

"No. I'd say it makes you more self-aware than most kids our age. Everyone thinks they're the best at everything. But that's logically not possible. Everyone needs to figure out what they are good at, then hopefully they get to do that for the rest of their lives. If you're doing what you're good at, I assume you'd be happy doing it."

"Yeah." There was a long pause where Chuck breathed in deeply, then let the air out slowly. "Deep conversation for a random weeknight after school, huh?"

"I guess so." He was going to come back around to me, and I still didn't know how to respond.

"So, come on…for real. What's bothering you? You know I just want to help."

"I know you do. I—" I paused, mind racing.

A car drove down one of the side streets, the headlights illuminated Chuck's face for a moment. He was looking at me, and I could see the worry on his face. I thought I'd done a better job of hiding the fact that something was wrong. Maybe I had with Mom and Dad, but hiding something from them and keeping a secret from Chuck were two different things entirely. Not only was Chuck with me more than any other person; he was also just good with people. He could tell what someone was feeling or thinking within a few minutes of meeting them.

"You should play poker, you know?" I said.

"Huh?"

"Poker. You're really good at reading people. That's probably what you're going to end up doing. Do what you're good at, right? Isn't that what they do in the movies? They try to figure out what cards the person has by watching their face and stuff. I bet you'd be a good poker player."

"I never thought of it. But that's not the point. Do you want to tell me, or not?"

"I do," I blurted it out before realizing what I was saying.

I gathered myself. Collected my thoughts. Chuck was okay with giving me the time.

"Listen. I *want* to tell you more than anything right now," I said. "That's what makes this hard. Have you ever wanted to tell someone something, but you just can't?"

"Oh, great. Not you, too?" Chuck leaned back on his elbows and looked up at the stars. The moon shone down on us at almost full. It seemed closer and brighter than usual.

"What do you mean, me too?"

"John. He said kinda the same thing to me today. He looked like he wanted to tell me something, and then just asked that same question. There's more he can't say."

"Yeah, he would," I said under my breath, but apparently it was loud enough for Chuck to hear.

"Oh, Jesus. What, are you two making out or something when no one else is around? That would be fucking gross. If it's that, please don't tell me. I'd rather not know."

I could hear him giggling and knew he was joking around. If that ever happened, Chuck would be the last person I'd tell.

"Oh shit, no. You're right. That *is* gross. Please… It's nothing like that. I don't know what he's talking about, just that he's been keeping secrets. I *do* want to tell you, Chuck. I just— I just can't. I really, really can't."

"You know I just want to help you. Whatever it is, I'm just trying to help."

"I know." I put my arm around his shoulders. "You're a good brother, and you're doing what you're good at. You could help me, but I can't tell you anything. You've got to trust me on that. Okay. For now, I've got to do this on my own."

He put his arm around me, and we gave each other a half a hug and looked up at the moon.

"All right. I'm going to go in. If you need me—"

"I know where you live. I know." I laughed.

Chuck stood up and went inside, leaving me alone with the darkness once again enveloping me and wrapping me inside a cold empty cocoon lacking any form of comfort.

<u>Chapter 11</u>

I never said anything about that meeting with Mr. Nightmare to anyone. As far as I knew, neither did Merrie. The only proof I had was the fact that everyone was still alive. I sure as hell had some nightmares about it, though. Long nightmares. Scary ones. Ones that woke me from a deep sleep. The dreams didn't just rouse me for a few minutes before I rolled over and fell back asleep; they woke me up screaming, sweating with the blankets wrapped around my legs, unsure of where I was. They were kind of nightmares where you knew you weren't going to sleep the rest of the night.

If there was a silver lining—because I'd quickly become the type of person who needed to find one anytime something bad happened—it was that real life was a lot scarier than the stories of the Nightmare Club. At least I wasn't giving anyone else extra points. I still wanted to win, after all.

I realized not long after the time we met Mr. Nightmare that he was someone to be truly scared of. The stories we told at night in the woods were just that…stories. They weren't real. They never would be real, and therefore, they weren't *that* scary. Mr. Nightmare wanted to keep the club going because we were going to produce more nightmares, but the opposite had happened for me. He scared me so much that make-believe terrors weren't as scary as they once were.

We kept the club going because we had to, but I knew Merrie and John didn't want it to continue. Still, I enjoyed going out there in the middle of the night and spending time with my friends. But the stories and the dreams didn't mean as much to me as they once had. The scores still mattered to me, but time with friends was just as important.

As the days got warmer and spring of eighth grade year turned into the summer before my freshman year of high school, weekly meetings of the Nightmare Club became easier to attend. It was good to get out in the warm air at night, walking out to the stop sign in shorts and a t-shirt instead of bundling up in a jacket with gloves and a winter hat. It reminded me of the first few meetings, before Mr. Nightmare. Things were different then.

The Nightmare Club hadn't really changed over the course of a year as much as I had. Merrie, too. And John. But the club stayed the same. We still

pulled names from a hat and told stories we hoped
would induce nightmares. It was still a great concept,
in theory. But the day the Nightmare Club changed for
good happened almost exactly a year after that first
meeting, when it was just Chuck, John, and myself.

Merrie and Marcus had become closer over the
year. She never told me she liked him, but I could tell
by the way she looked at him and how she talked about
him.

After we met at the corner on the night
everything changed, we started walking to The
Dwelling. I usually walked with Merrie. Halfway
down the street, Marcus came up from behind us and
slid in between to the two of us to talk to Merrie. I
didn't really care. I liked John and Merrie knew it,
although we never talked about it except for a few
passing comments here and there. I think we both
thought it was too close to talking about the one thing
that we weren't supposed to talk about.

But I worried about them getting close because
of the secret Merrie and I shared. Near slip-ups
happened from time to time when we were together.
She would start to mention something about that
afternoon, and I would stop her. Or I would bring
something up, and she would stop me. We watched out
for each other. As long as I was the person she was
closest to in the group, we could watch out for each
other. Merrie was my best friend. But if she had a slip
up with Marcus, if she started to talk about the day she

and I went into the woods to see The Dwelling in daylight, there would be no one there to stop her.

That worried me.

Maybe one day I'd mention it to her. But, so far, she'd been careful. We both had, and nothing bad had happened.

When Merrie and Marcus walked together, I slowed my pace a bit. I fell in between Chuck and John, who were both a few steps behind me.

"I'm telling you, Chuckie, you can be the starting third baseman next year. There is no doubt in my mind," John said.

"Why are you so sure?" Chuck said.

I didn't mind listening in to the end of high school baseball talk. Plus, I got to learn about some of the people I'd be seeing in the halls once we went back to school. I already knew a lot of kids in Chuck and John's grade because I was friends with them. But the more names I knew, the better the transition to 9th grade would be.

"Listen. Smitty graduated, so he's gone. Best catcher in the school, right?" John said. I could hear him getting excited and the pace of his words picked up. "The second-best catcher is O'Donnell, who was our starting third basemen. So next year, you're on the varsity team. I guarantee O'Donnell moves behind the plate, and that leaves third base open for you.

"You were the best on your team, and you have a better arm than any other infielder except O'Donnell.

Coach would be an idiot not to put you over there. I'm telling you, you just gotta come into spring ready to go. We'll go down to The Field starting in February, so you've got to get your bat speed up for tryouts. I'll pitch, and you can just hit every day for a month and half before tryouts even start. You'll blow everyone else away, and Coach probably already knows about your arm. Anna-banana doesn't mind shagging balls for us, do you?"

"Oh, course not." I laughed. "But I'm planning to be on the basketball team next year. Aren't they still playing games in February?"

"Oh, right, right." John put his arm around my shoulders and pulled my head against him, almost like putting me in a headlock. "Anna-banana is going to be a frosh pretty soon. Might even be class president by the end of the year."

"Yeah, right!" I was involved in school things, but we all knew I wasn't the kind of person who would run for class president.

"Bet she would probably run if you ran, John. What do you say?" Chuck said.

The three of us laughed. The only thing more unlikely than me running for class president was John doing it.

"Okay, okay. Neither of us will be class president. I was joking around, anyway. Point is, when I think about this time last year and where I am now, a lot has changed. I still have you guys. The five of us, I mean. But other than that, a lot has changed. It's only one year difference, but middle school to high school… It feels like a much bigger change than say fifth to sixth grade. Just a lot of change, you know?"

"Yeah, you're right," Chuck said. "For real. Like, when I think back on it, other than the five of us, there is a huge difference between last summer and this one. Like, there's the five of us, but my friends at school are totally different from my friends last year. I sit with different kids at lunch. There's some classes where I literally don't know anyone, even though we all came from only two different middle schools. There's definitely a lot of change."

"But Chuckie, Anna-banana here gets to have like a lesson in moving from middle school to high school before she actually has to do it. We can tell her about the crazy teachers, and she can know all the gossip and be the most popular kid because she knows you, me, and Marcus."

"He's right, Anna."

We turned down Red Bird. Merrie and Marcus were a few steps ahead of us, laughing about something. Merrie laughed loudly, and I noticed we were talking equally loud. When we used to walk these streets this late at night, it was a secret thing. We avoided the headlights of cars and did our best not to draw attention. One year later, we were comfortable. We didn't care who heard us. It might get us caught one of these days, but we hadn't been yet. On Saturday nights, the streets belonged to us.

As we stepped off the pavement, over the curb, and into the woods, I thought, even with all the drama and secrets we had, I wouldn't want to do this with any other group of kids. We were as close as family. I wouldn't change a thing. Later that night, things changed for good, anyway.

Chapter 12

We arrived at The Dwelling. Merrie had told the story the week before, so she took her place in the middle with the hat. John—not because it was his job, but because he enjoyed doing it—got the fire going while Chuck, Marcus, and I took our regular spots on the logs. Once the fire was going bright enough for us to see, we flipped our flashlights off, and Merrie looked to me.

From the back pocket of my shorts, I produced a small notebook. It was a miniature version of the one I kept under my bed. This smaller one only held the scores and nothing else. I carried the smaller one with me at all times in case anyone came to me with a dream. The job had originally been both mine and Chuck's, but without ever talking about it, I'd assumed the responsibilities on my own. Chuck still helped, and sometimes, Marcus or John would tell Chuck they had dreams when they saw him at school. But Chuck had never written anything in either notebook, so I'd become the one who tallied all the scores. I kind of liked it that way. I'd write down the points in a red pen and then circle the mark with a green one when it was in the big, official score book.

"Anyone have any dreams to report?" I asked, even though I knew the answer would be no. We'd got into the habit of asking about dreams from the previous week's story before we closed the book on it. Once the new name was drawn, it would be that person's week to collect points. "Okay, we're closing the book on Merrie's story then. She's currently in third place. Ten points behind Chuck, who is in second and seventeen points behind John, who is in first. Merrie is three points ahead of me and Marcus, who are tied for last place. Questions?"

The scores were skewed because John, Chuck, and Merrie had already told stories for this round. Only Marcus and I were up this week. When no one had any questions, I gave Merrie a nod, letting her know it was okay to proceed.

"Here we go." Merrie shook the hat and held it up above her head. She walked around the perimeter of logs behind us and stopped at Chuck.

Chuck reached up and grabbed one of the two slips of paper from the hat. He looked at it. "Anna."

I smiled. I'd had the idea for this story for a while and was anxious to give it a shot. It was a simple premise, but I thought I had worked it around in my head enough times to make it scary and put my own twist on it. I'd taken up reading horror books over the last year as a way to prepare myself for the club each week. I'd read a bunch of haunted house stories, but realized that sort of story didn't necessarily have to take place inside of one. So, I changed it a bit and was happy to finally get the chance to share it.

For the most part, our stories revolved around ghosts or physical monsters. Monsters that would chase after people. That and, of course, Mr. Nightmare. I wanted to combine the haunted house and the monster stories and make something totally new.

Sometimes we would introduce our story, but not always. I liked to start my stories out of the blue, when they weren't ready for it. No warning. No clearing of my throat. Just words. Right away. Even if it was just a quiet opening. Sometimes I stayed where I was instead of standing up and moving to the center of the circle. There was a lot of things you could do telling a story just by where you were physically in relation to the other people. I used that too, but I was thoughtful about it.

"This didn't happen recently," I said, still sitting in my spot on the log. The crickets had been chirping—almost screaming—but when I started to speak it was as if they seemed to quiet down and were listening, too. "It's an old story, one that was never shared with many people. You can't find it in the history books, and they don't make documentaries about it. We know about the Titanic because it was a ship that wasn't supposed to sink, and then it did. But how many other ships have sunk for reasons we will never know? The ocean is miles deep. There are things down there below the water where sunlight will never reach that we know nothing about. Humans may never know everything that is down there. When a ship goes down, it sinks to the bottom, and it joins those things: lost, forgotten. The events that brought that ship—and the people on it—to their eventual demise often get pulled to the bottom of the ocean with it."

We'd all taken on the strategy of making at least part of our stories seem like they could possibly be true. It was kind of cheap and I didn't like doing it, but for my story to work, it had to happen in the past so I felt like it was okay to throw a line in here and there to keep the possibility that it was a true story going. I kept my voice low on purpose for the preamble. I wanted them to lean in so they could only barely hear me. The crickets perked up once again as I spoke, but I kept my voice quiet, even making my friends strain to hear. Then I stood up to continue the story.

You won't find the story of the ship named the *Sunburst* in most history books. There are only mentions of it here and there. The official record simply reports the *Sunburst* was lost at sea. While that is technically true, there is a lot more to the story. It takes a bit of work to track it down, but the story is out there for those who want to find out about it.

The *Sunburst* left England bound for the American colonies in the early 1700s. It was filled with settlers—farmers mostly, and their families— headed for the New World and hopeful of what those distant lands would provide for them. It was September—not the greatest month to travel across the Atlantic because of the frequent storms that cut east across the ocean from New England. Knowing this and the final resting place of the *Sunburst,* one might assume the ship sank as a result of heavy seas from one of those storms coming off the coast of America, building as the came out over water until it was a monster storm that left the ship battered and beaten in its wake. And, like I said, it is *possible* that's exactly what happened to the *Sunburst*. But, if some of the rumors are to be believed, there was more going on with that ship.

James Lockwood was only eight years old when he boarded the *Sunburst.* He was with his father, his mother, and two younger sisters. Like everyone else boarding the ship with them, his family came from a long line of farmers over in England. But his father was having a hard time finding land to work. James's father inherited a small farm from *his* father, but it was split between him and his brother. When the brothers married and started families, it was near impossible to sustain both families on the single farm plot. One of the families needed to leave. The brothers agreed that James's father—the eldest of the two—would take his family to the New World. The price of land in the New World, along with fare for passage across the Atlantic, was less than it would have cost to find land in England. So, the adventurous elder brother left England, starry-eyed and hopeful that the new start would lead to great things for him and his young family.

Problems began as soon as they boarded the ship. They were inconsequential things to begin with and therefore, no one worried about them. But looking back at James's story in its entirety shows us the problems were there from the beginning.

It was a gray September day when James and his family boarded that ship. His first impression of the ship that would become his home until they arrived in the colonies as many as eight weeks later, was that the boat was as dark as the clouds above them. When he traversed the ramp up to the main deck, he noticed the wooden beast groaned and creaked with each step. With his father in front of him and his mother behind, a sister's hand in each of his own, James stepped onto the deck for the first time.

He'd been on a few ships before, but nothing this big and sea worn. There was a difference between ships that remained in and around English waters and the ones that made numerous trips back and forth across the unforgiving ocean. The *Sunburst* had seen more water than most ships. The deck felt like it was held together with springs and knitting needles instead of nails and cleats. The ship was anchored and the sea calm in spite of the clouds. Yet, when James stepped on board, the entire ship moved with each step. When he moved, the solid wood beneath his foot bounced up and down in a slow steady motion. He took a few more steps, harder, to be sure and was certain he felt the movement.

James looked to his father, watching his reaction to see if he noticed the same movement under his feet, but the man didn't show any sign that things were off. He glanced back at his mother. She always had a sixth sense for when something was wrong, but her first few steps on board didn't have any reaction apart from what James would consider normal. His sisters, however, immediately looked at their feet when they touched the strange floor of the ship. They looked at James and then back at the strange sponge-like floor. The three children looked at their feet and stepped as if walking through a muddy field instead of the solid wood deck of a massive ship. None of the three said anything.

His father went ahead. James fell back and pulled his sisters closer to him.

"What's wrong with your feet?" he asked the girls.

"Strange," was the older one's reply. It was all either of them said before James' father hurried them along and they found the space below deck where they would live for the next six weeks.

I had been standing near the middle of the circle next to the fire and hadn't moved much for the first part of the story. When coming up with the story I had the idea to move back and forth behind my friends so my voice would move around behind them and give the impression they were on a ship floating at sea. I wasn't sure if it would produce the desired effect, but I wanted to try it out. So when I continued the story, I started pacing as I did so.

James didn't know if he was the only one to notice something was not quite right with the ship. He didn't talk to many of the other people making the trip, even the few other kids around his age. But once they were out at sea, he, and all of the other kids, had the run of the ship. With nowhere else to go, they roamed free, trying not to get in trouble and having to hear about it from any adults in the area when they went somewhere they weren't supposed to. While some of the kids ran and played, James wandered, silently. He listened to the adults talking about plans in the colonies. He heard everything because he kept to himself and didn't bother anyone. He even overheard a man talking about the monsters that were supposed to lurk just under the surface of the sea to their north. That, the man said, was the reason for their more southerly course. He listened in as a man and a woman grunted and moaned while they wrestled in the cargo area. But he also heard the ship.

Most of the others were busy with the day-to-day activities and just simply didn't notice. The ship had a voice of its own. For the first week or two, the ship sounded like a series of rhythmic creaks as it rose up and down on shallow swells of a calm ocean. To anyone who took the time to listen, they would have realized there was more to it than just the sounds of wood and nails sliding and twisting in place. The ship had a voice, and James heard it speak to him as clear as he overheard adults talking about their worries of attacks in the colonies. You just had to listen.

The first time he heard the ship speak to him was in the bowels of the ship, surrounded by an uncounted number of people either sleeping or pretending to sleep, James was lying awake well after dark. His eyes were open, though he couldn't tell due to the complete lack of light below deck. As usual, he listened.

In his immediate surroundings were the sounds of his father and mother, both snoring as they slept. He'd never known they snored until this trip. He was always asleep before them and woke up after them. At home, they slept far enough away that if he woke up during the night, he couldn't hear them. The ship forced them to sleep in close quarters, and now he heard it all. His sisters weren't snoring, but he could hear their slow steady breathing. Other than the first day when the wood felt wrong, his sisters never noticed anything else strange about the ship.

The wood still felt wrong to James. Initially, he had passed it off as just his body getting used to the way it felt. Part of him even wondered if he'd made the whole thing up when he first boarded. But then the ship spoke to him. And the voice of the ship wasn't just in his head.

"Get off," the ship said in a fleeting whisper between the splash of waves and a gust of wind. The words were hidden between the creaks and groans, between the snores and breaths around him. Hidden between everything, but James heard.

"Hello," James said quietly, almost to the point of being inaudible. "Who is that?"

He wasn't scared, though, even when he asked the question, he knew the answer. He lay still. Held his breath. Listened.

"Get off me," again the ship's words could have been waves or wind, part of the constant noise of life at sea. But James knew better—it was the ship.

James didn't have to prove it to anyone because he didn't want to tell anyone he could hear the ship speaking. He'd seen people get put away for being crazy and saying things others deemed insane. He was certain telling anyone—even just his father and mother—that the ship had spoken to him was enough to see him locked up at least until they arrived in the New World. So, he kept it to himself.

Still, each night he sat up after most of the ship had gone to sleep, when it was dark and the people were silent. When the only sounds were outside the ship, or of the ship. In those hours, the ship spoke to him. The message was always the same.

"Get off me."

James spoke back to the ship, tried to reason with it. He explained why the people on the ship were there. He told it how the ship was helping all of the people. But the ship never changed its stance. It wanted them off. The longer this lasted—the simple request that James could not grant—the more it weighed on him. He grew weary of the burden the ship was putting on him. He told his parents he was having trouble sleeping at night, which was true. He just left out the reason he wasn't sleeping.

In his dark conversations with the ship, James explained the fact that he would get off the ship if he could but that his parents wouldn't let him. He was just a child, he explained, and if he had control over the situation then, of course, he would help. But there was nothing he could do. The ship didn't speak in response to that. James saw it as progress.

September became October and the crisp nights
turned cold. The below deck area his family and many
others used grew warmer than the air above deck. But
James shivered during the night. He continued to speak
with the *Sunburst* each night, though the ship still
refused to change its tune.

"Get off me."

With each request from James for more
information, he was met with the same reply.

"Get off me."

The trip neared its end. James had failed to
make any human friends. Even his sisters and parents
managed to make friends with a few of the other
families making the trip. His only friend—the thing he
had spoken with for hours every night when it was just
the two of them—was the ship. With the rest of people
on board rejoicing at the chance to get off less than two
weeks from now, James felt a sadness. He didn't get
much back from the *Sunburst*, but still, he would miss
his friend.

Less than a week out from landfall, James
heard his friend, this time during the day. He almost
missed the sound of the ship's voice because he wasn't
ready for it or listening. But once he caught the end of
what sounded like a word, James managed to find
himself a quiet place. He lay down like he did every
night, his face close to the exposed wood beneath him.

"What did you say?" James asked. "It sounded
different."

"Get off me," the ship said. Then, after a pause, it said, "You safe. Follow me."

James' eyes widened as the wood beneath him vibrated from left to right. James followed the sensation along the lower deck and then up the stairs to the top deck, and out to the bow of the ship. He was the only one there, staring westward at water, land possibly somewhere beyond that. The wind blew his hair. In the weeks he'd spent on the ship, he'd never been out to the bow before. James stood at the very front of the ship, the water down below him, the ship splashing and cutting into it, the bow rising and falling against the waves. James held his position looking out at the water and then turned back when he heard shouting.

"Water!" someone yelled

"We're taking on water!" Others stood, turned and looked, then made a sprint for the ramp that led below deck.

James saw his father go down with the other men. He looked for his mother and sisters but couldn't find them. For a moment, he thought about running back into the ship to look for them. He even stutter stepped and almost took off running, but something stopped him. He retreated back to his position on the bow, clinging to the rail behind him as he watched chaos unfold in front of him.

"Get off me," the ship said. But it wasn't directed at James. He knew that now.

There was the sound of cracking wood and rushing water, sounds that should never exist on a ship in the middle of the ocean. People ran and screamed. James watched as the boat ripped itself in half. Splinters flew in all directions. The back half of the ship sank faster than it should have, almost as if it was pulled down to the dark cavernous depths below.

Most of the people on the ship were on the back half because James only saw a handful left on the front section. The rest of his family were not among them. The deafening sound of more wood creaking and breaking echoed around him.

"Turn," the ship said.

He could hear the ship even above the screaming and bedlam surrounding him. He was scared, but James did as his friend asked, tears dripping down his face when the ship exploded behind him. His back was pelted with splinters and shards of split wood.

Most of the front part of the *Sunburst* was pulled down below the surface as fast and hard as the back section had been. James caught a glimpse of a man's face as the ship went under. The man's eyes were wide and wild, his lips pulled back in a grimace of fear. Then he disappeared below the surface. The ship broke apart, pieces of it sinking below the surface of the water. Within a few minutes, the entire thing was under water. The *Sunburst*—except for the piece James stood on—was gone.

Standing on a piece of the ship that should not have been able to float on its own, James scanned his surroundings. Somehow, he'd stayed out of the water and dry even as the entire boat and all of the people on it were pulled down into the depths. There were no survivors, no floating shards of wood, no scattered bits of cargo.

James was able to sit on his small piece of the *Sunburst.* He folded his legs underneath him, wondering what would happen now.

"Just us," the remaining piece of the ship said.

"Yes," James said. Then he cried.

I knew the story of James and the *Sunburst* didn't have a satisfying conclusion. In the Nightmare Club, we'd grown accustomed to knowing what happened to the characters in the story and I purposefully left it open ended, hoping that not knowing would produce a few nightmares. Because of that, I let the silence hang for as long as I could. No one knew if I was going to continue or not, so they stayed silent, waiting or the rest of the story. I paced back and forth behind them, like I had for the bulk of the story, still—hopefully—making them feel like they were on the small piece of the ship with James, floating by himself while the rest of the ship and everything on it had somehow been pulled deep into the ocean.

I made them wait, hoping that the next day I'd find out they all had dreams about my monster ship. When John broke the silence, I realized no one would be thinking about my story. He opened his mouth, and that was the moment the Nightmare Club changed.

Chapter 13

"I wanted to let Anna-banana tell her story before I brought this up," John said.

I don't know if my groan was audible or not, but Chuck's was.

"What is it?" Chuck asked. "That was a really good story, Anna. I liked it."

"Oh, of course, Anna-b. It was awesome," John said. He looked at me, and I could tell in his eyes he believed it. But he also had something to get off his chest. "Listen. I didn't want to do this before, because, you know, I just— Because of what happened before, I didn't want it to be like I was taking your time or whatever. And you guys always told me before that…that I should tell you when these kinds of things happen. So I wanted to tell you, and I didn't really get a chance today. That's all."

"John," I said. "It's fine. It's really not a big deal. I got to tell my story, and we did say that. So let's hear it."

"Well, it's been a long time. Like a very long time since I've seen him. You know…*him*." John held his hands out in front of him.

We all knew who he was talking about. I tried to shoot a look at Merrie, but she was watching John. And I didn't want anyone else to see.

"We know, John. We know." Marcus stepped forward into the light. The reflections of the flames danced across his face. His expression serious. "So, what is it?"

"Well, like I said… it's been a while since Mr. Night—"

Merrie came at him like she was going to hit him. I thought she would, too, with the speed she moved toward him. But she slowed up at the last second. Instead of hitting him, she put her hand on his chest and pulled him toward her in a sort of half-hug. "John, I thought you said you weren't supposed to talk about it because bad things could happen," Merrie said, loudly.

"I…well, yes. He did say that. But nothing happened the last two times we talked about it, right? I just assumed nothing would happen this time, either." John shrugged. "Probably just a bullshit threat, anyway. Right?"

I knew I needed to help Merrie. No one knew what we knew. Chuck and Marcus probably wanted to hear what John had to say. I needed to swing their thoughts in a different direction.

"Yeah, but, I mean…" I moved toward John and put a hand on his shoulder, too. "You said something would happen to one of us if you said too much, so we wouldn't want to test it, would we? I know it's eating away at you, but if he said not to mention it, wouldn't it be best if you follow that rule?"

He looked to me and then at Merrie, then up at Chuck and Marcus.

"Yeah, they're probably right, John," Marcus said. It didn't matter what Chuck was thinking then. We'd been able to get Marcus on our side, and that would be enough. "Is there a way to get the point across without talking about it directly? I mean, is your life in danger? Or any of ours?"

I wasn't sure about this tactic, but Mr. Nightmare had been pretty clear with Merrie and I. We couldn't talk to anyone about him or tell them anything about what he had said to us. John was smart, though. Maybe he could figure out a way around that, to get the message across to us without actually talking about Mr. Nightmare and the things he'd said to him.

But that wasn't really in the spirit of what Mr. Nightmare wanted, was it? I wasn't so sure about John telling us this information in a roundabout way—or any other way—to be honest. If there was one thing I knew about Mr. Nightmare, it was that he wasn't the type of guy who would enjoy a bunch of kids looking for loopholes in his rules.

The problem was, John liked Marcus's idea.

"Yeah, I guess I could tell you guys what he said without really telling you it was him. That wouldn't count, right? If I told you about something my dad said a few nights ago, I wouldn't really be talking about that other guy. Just, you know, talking about my dad."

"Yeah," Marcus and Chuck said almost at the same time. They stepped closer to us, and we ended up huddled around John.

I shot Merrie another look. This time she caught it, and we both shook our heads. We couldn't let John do this.

Merrie stepped in. "Maybe we shouldn't though, just in case. We never know what could happen. If he has the ability to appear in your room, John, who knows what else he could really do? And, like you said about his…his f-face. Maybe there is more to him than just some guy after all. We should respect that, and he hasn't hurt any of us yet, so maybe we should do what he wants."

Maybe Merrie and Marcus getting closer could be a good thing. Maybe he would side with Merrie on all of this. He opened his mouth to speak, but Chuck, who always had an opinion but had been remarkably quiet, finally chimed in.

My heart sank.

"You two know more than what you're saying," Chuck said, looking at Merrie first and then at me.

"What do you mean?" John said. His eyes narrowed.

"What I mean is, they know something they're not telling us. Right? I'm not mad. I'm sure there is a good reason for you keeping it from us. I love all you guys. I'd do anything for any of you, and I trust you all with my life. That being said, I think we need to go along with what Merrie and Anna are saying here. If they do know something, it will all come out eventually, maybe when its safe. If they don't, then I'm wrong and we're still being careful by not talking about Mr. Nightmare. Let's just clean up and head out. Anna told a hell of a story, but I have a feeling no one is going to be dreaming about it tonight. And that sucks. But maybe our meetings are bigger than just the scores we write down in that notebook."

I had never really thought of the Nightmare Club as a group that needed a leader. The only leader we ever talked about was whoever led in points on any given week. But as Mr. Nightmare slowly changed what we were over time, maybe that was exactly what we needed. And Chuck had stepped up out of nowhere and taken the role. He'd always been good at reading people, but the fact that he'd figured out—sort of—the secret that Merrie and I thought we'd kept so well hidden was proof of his ability. We needed someone who knew how to read people like that if Mr. Nightmare was going to continue to force us to keep secrets from each other. I was just surprised Chuck had taken the initiative.

We cleaned up The Dwelling, put out the fire as best we could, and filed out of the woods. When we got back to the street, John and Chuck walked in front. The rest of us were just behind them.

Merrie grabbed my arm so Marcus couldn't see, and walked slower. At first, Marcus did too, then he must have noticed we needed some time. He gave a quick nod and picked up his pace to join Chuck and John. When he caught up to the them, he said something I couldn't hear. All three looked back at Merrie and I.

We waved, smiled.

They turned back around picking up their pace while we slowed ours.

I knew she wanted to talk to me. I was worried about what we could—or couldn't—say, too. I also fretted that what John had said at the end of our meeting was already too much and it no longer mattered what we did or didn't talk about now.

"I don't know what to say," Merrie said, echoing my thoughts.

"I know. Me too."

The boys turned off Red Bird Drive. I saw Chuck glace back at us before they made the turn and were out of sight.

"Is there anything we can do, even?" Merrie said.

"I don't think so. Chuck figured it out. The way we were talking, he must have figured out that we were letting on. If there is one thing he's good at, its speaking his mind and addressing the issue in the moment. He knew after that day something was up with me, and maybe he connected all the pieces. Other than that, I think I've acted pretty normal around everyone. The weird way I was acting back then when we came out here, plus the way we acted tonight must have been enough for him to figure it all out I'm sure of it."

"Well, I guess that's a good thing then. If he knows we tried to stop John from talking about it and he knew something happened that we can't talk about, then he's managed to keep everyone safe."

"I hope. Unless it's too late and John said more than he should have, and Chuck was a little too late figuring it all out."

"Then we're screwed," Merrie finished my thought.

We made the same turn off of Red Bird the boys had made a few moments earlier and walked in silence for a while. Talking about what had happened to us in code and only peripherally was difficult, and there was only so much we could say. I didn't trust myself to continue the conversation without slipping up. If we were going to talk about anything, it had to be something other than the end of the meeting. I didn't know what Merrie was thinking but guessed it was the same thing.

"It's going to get lost in all of this, Anna, but that story was really good." Merrie evidently wanted to change the subject too. "I don't know how many dreams are going to come out of it now, because of all this, but I loved it. It was more than just a scary story. It's a story about friendship and loneliness as well as being just plain old scary and creepy."

"Huh. You know, I never even really thought about that when I was coming up with it. But I guess you're right. I just wanted to do a different kind of story than what we usually tell, but was still weird and scary and stuff."

"Well, you did that," Merrie said. "But all your stories have, like, a deeper meaning to them, I've noticed. You could be a writer, for real. I'm not just saying that. All your stories are a little bit different and interesting."

"That's awesome." I smiled. "Thanks for saying that."

We walked the rest of the way in silence. Merrie by my side, we turned the final corner and saw the three boys standing at the corner in a circle looking at their feet and kicking the gravel. We approached and John took a step forward.

"Just waiting and make sure you two were okay," he said.

"We are," I said.

"All right. I know you're keeping us safe."

I nodded.

"Yup," said Merrie.

The awkward silence lasted a few seconds. I think they wanted Merrie or I to say more, but we both knew the best thing to say was nothing at all.

"All right, so I guess it's done then," Chuck said. "Anna, good story tonight. I really liked it."

Everyone nodded or gave some sort of verbal agreement. Then we turned to leave.

They all thought the matter was over, but I knew Chuck would have more questions for me on the short walk back to the house.

"You can't tell me what happened to you two, right?' Chuck said the moment we were out of earshot.

I said nothing.

"I get it. But I'm assuming I was on the right track back there. We just have to keep John's mouth shut about all this until we figure it all out. I don't know how, but we will somehow."

I still said nothing as we walked up the driveway.

"Thanks for keeping us all safe. It actually feels better knowing that you and Merrie have our backs. John gets excited and nervous about stuff sometimes. You know how he is. I'm sure he feels better he's not actually doing all of this alone anymore. Anyway, thanks again."

Chuck stopped at my bedroom window and helped me back inside. The night was over.

No one dreamed about the *Sunburst* or James, the boy who could hear the words of the monstrous ship. None of the others dreamed about Mr. Nightmare, either. At least they didn't say anything, if they did. I did though. I dreamed about Mr. Nightmare standing over me, a light shining right on the thing that doubled as his face. The whole time he was yelling at me, telling me we were too late. We hadn't stopped John and hadn't protected our group from some terrible accident. But it was just a dream. That was the night I'll never forget.

Chapter 14

July had turned to August and we were getting ready to go back to school. John, Chuck, and Marcus were heading into tenth grade. I'd be going to the high school for ninth grade, and Merrie was going to eighth grade. She was only two months younger than me, but because of when our birthdays fell, I was in a grade above her. I'd miss not seeing her in the halls, but like the older boys had told us, everyone you see and are friends with changes from eighth grade to ninth. Still, I knew Merrie would always be my friend.

We still had a few weeks before the start of school. That Saturday started normally enough. Chuck and I woke up, had breakfast, and did our chores like usual. Mom was moving from room to room, doing the stuff she normally did. Dad was outside doing whatever it was he did outside all day on the weekends. When I sat down in the living room waiting for Chuck to be ready to go, Dad came in, kicked off his shoes and sat with me.

"Are you two headed to The Field today?" Dad said.

He stretched out in the chair that was lovingly known as Dad's chair. Other people had sat in it, of course. On rainy summer days when Dad was at work and we couldn't go outside, it became Chuck's chair. If John, Merrie, and Marcus came over on a Friday night after a trip to the video store for movie night, it became Marcus's chair. But most of the time it was Dad's chair.

"Yeah. Like always." I had my sneakers in one hand and socks on my feet ready to go, just waiting for Chuck to finish up his shower.

"Well, that makes it sound like you don't like it. Like always." Dad leaned forward.

"Oh. No, no. I mean, The Field is fine. And I love the company. We just run out of things to do sometimes. You know, by this point in the summer all the good ideas are kind of used up. John usually comes up with some new things to do."

"Oh yeah. I understand that. Summer vacation when I was a kid was totally different for me. You know Grandma and Grandpa's lake house?"

I nodded. My grandparents had a lake house a few hours north in Wisconsin. We went there from time to time, but Dad worked too many hours for us to spend a lot of time there. My uncle, Bobby, and his family were there a lot and if we went too, it would be overcrowded. Besides, I'd rather be home than at the lake house. Dad wasn't much of a talker at the dinner table or when we were all together in a group. But when he got you one on one and had something to say, he loved to tell stories. I guess Chuck and I were following in his footsteps. When he started talking about the lake house, I knew I was getting a story.

"Well, we spent almost the entire summer there. We'd come back home a few days a week just to check on the house and take care of the lawn, but most of the summer was spent up there. Anyway, because of that, I hardly saw the friends I had in our neighborhood and from school over the summer. The neighbors we had at the lake were the same as us. They spent most of the summer there at the lake, and they had kids that were around the same age as me and Uncle Bobby. They became our summer friends.

"I only saw them or talked to them in the summer. When we closed up the lake house for the winter, we said goodbye. Then I wouldn't see them again until the following June. I had my home friends and my summer friends, and that's just the way it was. I felt lucky in a way because I had these two different groups of friends.

"But I also always worried that I was missing out on things. With my home friends, I missed out on the stuff that happened over the summer. When we got back to school, they were still my friends, but it took a few weeks for us to find the common ground that we'd had in June. The same thing was true with my summer friends. But they always changed a lot more over the school year, as did I. But we still found stuff to do and became close. I still have a few summer friends I talk to. And a few neighborhood friends, too. But I'm not as close to them because I missed out on those times. I'm glad you and Chuck have a group of friends you see year-round. It's good to have that, I think."

"Yeah. I think," I said. "I know things change, but we're pretty close. I hope the five of us are all still friends when we're older. We can still hang out and get together, even if we all have families of our own and stuff. It would be good."

I turned my head as Chuck walked into the room, socks hanging over his shoulder sneakers in his hand.

"Hey," Chuck said.

"I was just telling Anna that I think it's great you two have a good group of friends," Dad said. "I didn't always have that."

"We do. I think we have a really good crew. I hope we stick together. I think we will," Chuck said.

"Well, you two are off, I assume. One good thing about dead grass is that I don't have to spend all day Saturdays cutting it. Have a good day, guys, and I'll see you later." Dad got up and went into the kitchen, either to find Mom or to use the bathroom.

Chuck raised his eyebrows at me and smiled.

"Ready?" I said, and smiled back at him.

"Yep, and I had an idea about the little problem we have," Chuck said.

He put a finger to his mouth, warning me not to ask any questions until we were out of ear shot. He tied his shoes and ran out of the house. I was two steps behind him. We kept running down the driveway and didn't stop until we hit the street.

"What is it? You mean Nightmare Club problems?" I asked.

"Yep. It happens to John at night, right? What about a sleepover?"

My heart skipped a beat. I'd been in John's bedroom before, a handful of times, usually just for short periods of time. The thought of spending the night there filled my stomach with butterflies.

"Well, for you maybe." I was trying to sound casual. "But there is no way Mom and Dad would be okay with me spending the night in a boy's bedroom. Even if it was just John. And Merrie's parents? Sleeping over at a high school kid's house?"

"I thought of that. I don't really have a solution other than to come up with a good reason for why we have to do it or lie to them all. But I figured it wouldn't hurt to talk about it today and see what the others thought, and get some ideas."

"Yeah, I agree. It is a good idea. Especially if we can see…you know…"

"Yeah. It would be worth it so we could all be on the same page."

It was shocking to see how quickly we'd all grown accustomed to speaking in this kind of code. We knew what we were talking about and never once mentioned Mr. Nightmare. Whenever we talked about him, we said the same kind of things. Being on the same page meant we all knew the same information about him. And we usually referred to him as 'our friend' or a paused sentence and then used the words 'you know.' But we never talked about what John saw or what Merrie and I saw. Everything was about the future and how we could change the current trajectory we were on. We all knew we needed to flip the tables on him and were trying to figure out a way to do that, so he wouldn't hold so much power over us.

We got to The Field and found Merrie and John already hiding out in one of the dugouts. It was early, but the sun was hot and the dugouts provided shade and let the breeze in. The only other shady place we had was under the trees by the basketball courts, but we had to sit on the ground over there.

"Hey guys," Chuck said. "Where's Marcus?"

He directed his question to both of them but looked at Merrie when he asked it. Apparently, I wasn't the only one who noticed they'd been spending more and more time together.

"Dunno," John said, and shrugged.

"I'm sure he'll be along," Merrie said. "He said he'd be here this morning. You guys ready for tonight. Could be anyone this week."

"Yup, I'm ready," Chuck said. "Ready to take the lead back."

John looked at Chuck and laughed. "With your stories? I don't think so. Anna-banana here would be in the lead if I didn't fuck everything up a couple of weeks ago. That ship story was my favorite of all the stories so far. For real."

"Yeah, I loved that one," Merrie said.

"Do you two share story ideas?" John pointed at me and Chuck.

"No way," I said and made a gagging face.

"Oh, okay." John laughed and put his hands up.

Chuck and Merrie laughed too.

"No, seriously," I said. "It's not that I don't like Chuck's opinion. We talk about stuff all the time. But with the stories, if he knows what I'm talking about or I know parts of his story, it takes the mystery away. There's no way the other person would have dreams about it that way. So, we definitely don't share any story ideas."

"But we do share other ideas. I might have an idea to deal with our other problem with, you know...*our friend.*"

"Chuck, it's not nice to talk about Marcus when he's not here." John kept a straight face, then grinned.

"Not that friend. Our *other* friend."

"Well, what's the idea?" Merrie said.

"We should wait for Marcus, I think," John said.

Chuck nodded. "Yeah. You guys want me to go get him?"

I could tell Chuck was anxious to let the others in on his idea and wanted share right now whether or not Marcus was there.

"Let's wait a few more minutes," John said. "If he doesn't show, you can run up there or we can all go."

We sat around in the dugout for a while, John in between Merrie and me. The three of us took turns throwing gravel stones through the fence without hitting any of the metal wires. Chuck stood at the dugout entrance. He half-paid attention to our conversation and kept looking out toward the street Marcus would come down on his way to The Field.

About fifteen minutes later, Chuck couldn't wait any longer. I was actually proud of him for waiting as long as he had.

"I'm gonna go get him," Chuck said, standing at the gate leading out of the baseball field.

The three of us looked up but didn't move. I think we all knew it wouldn't be long before he had to go get Marcus. We were just waiting for the when.

"Sounds good," John said. "We'll wait here for you. Then we can pow-wow about how to take care of our problem. I'm excited to hear your idea."

"It could work, I think," I said, but the gate clanged shut and Chuck was already gone.

"You think we might be able to get rid of our problem?" John said.

The three of us—Merrie, John, and I—had spent a lot more time together the last few weeks. We knew we couldn't talk about Mr. Nightmare, but I think for John, knowing that we'd experienced the same thing made him feel less alone. So he wanted to stay with us. Maybe he just felt better knowing what he'd seen was real.

"I think it's the best idea we've had in the last two weeks," I said.

Not that anyone really had any ideas to get Mr. Nightmare out of hiding. It was hard to describe what you wanted to do when you couldn't talk about a thing. If we could talk about it and pool our ideas, maybe we could come up with a plan. By threatening us the way he did, Mr. Nightmare had isolated us so that we couldn't work together.

We kept tossing the small stones through the chain-link fence. You only got a point if it made it through without making a sound. To no one's surprise, John was winning. We'd been at it for maybe ten minutes when we heard sirens off in the distance.

We didn't do anything at first. Sirens in the distance were not anything unusual, so we kept playing. Merrie was getting better and John had missed a few throws in a row, so the scores were getting tighter. But the sirens grew louder and closer. We gave a look at the exit to the dugout but still didn't get up. It

was only when the sirens sounded like they were in
The Field parking lot that we left the dugout to
investigate.

We came around the corner and looked in the
direction of the noise, but there was nothing to see in
the parking lot or on any of the streets that we could
see. We knew whatever had happened, it was close by.

"Come on," Merrie said. "Let's go see what's
going on."

"Probably a house fire or maybe a gas leak,"
John speculated as we pushed our way through the
gate.

We crossed the grass area to the parking lot and
headed along the sidewalk in the direction of the sirens
which had stopped drawing closer. We turned left on
one of the side streets, and the sirens stopped. By then
we could see the red and blue lights flashing on the
sides of some of the houses.

I realized it was coming from the direction of
Marcus's house. I looked at Merrie and John, and their
expressions told me they had come to the same
realization.

"Come on," I said and broke into a jog.

Not a full-on sprint because, if nothing had
happened to Marcus, I didn't want to seem like the
idiot who sprinted all the way to his house. But when
Merrie and John started running and pulled up beside
me, we all picked up our pace. We sprinted up the
street and around the corner, looking between houses

for any sign of what was going on. We cut through a few backyards and spilled out into the road, almost headlong into a police cruiser parked on the side of the road, lights flashing. There was a second police car and an ambulance. Marcus was standing on the side of the road, arms crossed, staring at something on the ground behind the ambulance that I couldn't see. There were tears on his cheeks.

"Marcus!" I yelled, out of breath.

He looked over at me, and his eyes widened. The police officer with him looked up at me, too. He said something to Marcus, then he tried to grab him by the shoulder. But Marcus slipped out of his grip and ran over to where we were. He came right to me and wrapped his arms around me, then pulled me tight against him.

"I-I don't know what happened, Anna. I come out of the house and he was just...just there. I ran back in and called—"

"What do you mean?"

I pushed Marcus off of me and ran over to the other side of the ambulance. The cop that had tried to stop Marcus from running over blocked my path. He grabbed my arm and tried to stop me. I twisted out of his grip and got around the corner of the ambulance. There was blood all over the street—lots of it.

In the middle of the viscus pool, Chuck lay motionless. His leg was twisted back in a way legs weren't supposed to. His head was craned to one side, so unnatural looking, it made me gag. I had to suppress a shout when I got a step closer and my gaze travelled from his broken body to his face and saw his lifeless eyes staring back at me. I took another step toward my brother, but was stopped when the cop wrapped his massive arms around me and pulled me back.

"Honey, come on. You don't want to see that," he said.

He was right. I didn't want to see it. But he was my brother—my best friend. Even though I didn't *want* to see it, I *had* to see it. I fought him off a second time, but his grip was too strong and he forced me away.

"Chuck!" I shouted. As he pushed me back, the ambulance blocked my view of Chuck's body so I couldn't see him anymore.

"Let them help him," the cop said. "Stay with your friends. What is your phone number so we can contact your parents?"

"What?" I had heard his words, but they weren't registering.

Merrie and Marcus put their arms around me. I think I hugged them back. I couldn't be sure. John gave the police officer our home number.

From that point on, everything was just flashes and images in my head. Things moved fast, but time went slow. There were points I remember clearly, like sitting on the side of the road after the ambulance pulled away—Dad and Chuck inside. John, Merrie, and Marcus had their arms around me. Mom was in hysterics talking to the police officer in the middle of the road. I remember thinking I should go try to help her calm down. But inside I was feeling the same thing she was; we were just showing it differently.

Eventually, Mom and I got a ride to the hospital with one of the police officers. I remember sitting in the waiting room, wanting news about Chuck's condition. Dad sat between Mom and I, his arms around both of us. I remember in that moment praying to God—something I'd never done seriously—asking him to save my brother and make him okay.

At some point the doctor came in. They pulled us into a smaller room so we could talk privately. I knew that wasn't good. I knew he was dead when I saw the way Chuck lay on the street in from of Marcus' house.

"I'm very sorry." The doctor looked at all of us. We were all crying. We all already knew in our heads; he was just confirming the fact. "We did everything we could, but he didn't make it."

Mom wailed again and kicked the wall. Dad tried to console her, but she pushed him off. She collapsed to the floor, whimpering and sniffling, curled into a ball. I sat in the corner of the room, my head in my arms, crying.

The day ended. Chuck was dead.

But the hard part was still coming.

Chapter 15

I woke up the next morning wishing it had all been a dream. There was no way Chuck could be dead. It wasn't possible. It was a strange trip home from the hospital. There were only three of us in the car. Four people in our family, but only three of us made the trip home. Sleep was a struggle to attain and restless. Every moment I was awake, sadness crashed over me.

When I woke up, I stayed in bed. I didn't want to see anyone. There were footsteps outside my room; I could tell by the way the feet met the floor that it was Dad. He was up, but the TV wasn't on. He wasn't doing yard work or finding something to keep busy. He was just awake. Alone. Quiet.

It was afternoon when there was a knock at my door.

"Yeah," I said, quietly. It was not my normal voice.

"You shouldn't just stay in bed all day," Dad said. He pushed my door open a few inches and stuck his head in.

"Well, I want to."

"I know. Me too. Your Mom, as well. We all do. It's not going to be a fun time around here today. And we have some things we have to get ready for…for what happens next. I don't want you to just sit here. John lost his best friend. And Merrie and Marcus lost a friend too. They need you as much as you need them right now," Dad said still just standing in the door.

I felt myself getting ready to cry again at the thought of seeing them.

"We will be here for you, and I know you know that, but sometimes it's not our parents that help us through life as much as our friends. Grandma and Grandpa will be here, but not until tonight. You should see your friends. I called John's house and talked to his mom. He's at The Field; probably with the others. But they need their friend right now. You don't have to be strong for them, Anna. Just let them be there for you, and you for them. Okay? At least *think* about going. Okay?"

He was waiting for some kind of recognition that I'd heard him. I didn't want to do anything—see my friends, respond, or even breathe.

"Okay," I said.

"That's all I ask." He pulled the door shut.

I thought back to the day before—to any of the days before this day. Some mornings, I'd hop out of bed eager to get in the shower before Chuck, so I could wait for him. And we'd rush off to The Field, trying to be the first ones there. Any day, even the day I'd met Mr. Nightmare, was better than this one.

The police stopped by our house late, after we got home from the hospital. I was in my room, and Dad asked him to talk on the porch instead of coming inside. He didn't know I'd overheard the whole conversation. They were ruling it a hit and run. Marcus had left his house and saw Chuck just lying on the ground. He ran over the check on him, at first thinking Chuck was messing around. Then he ran back in and called 911 once he realized it was real.

Another neighbor hadn't seen Chuck get hit, but had heard the impact. They had seen the car drive off moments later and had also run into their house to call 911. The timing of this 'accident' was not lost on me. Chuck had come up with an idea that might help us confront Mr. Nightmare and, within a few hours of telling me about it, he was dead. It was too strange to be a coincidence. I wondered if the others had made the same connection.

I also wondered who was to blame for this accident. Was it Chuck? Or me? Or had John slipped up? Maybe it was Merrie spending a bit too much time and opening up to Marcus. I couldn't let it eat away at me, though. I had to push it to the side. If it was Mr.

Nightmare, the only person I could be mad at was Mr. Nightmare. I realized, I needed to talk to my friends and forced myself out of bed.

I didn't shower, didn't do any chores, and didn't sit for breakfast. Dad handed me a granola bar on my way out the door.

"It's a hard decision to make, but also a good one, I think," he said.

He was sad, heartbroken. It was plastered on his face. Yet, even through his own heartbreak, he was doing what he could for me. I respected that. I always loved my dad, but this was different. Mom and I were a mess, and he was holding everything together for us, because he had to. It showed me what kind of person he was, and that inspired me, hoping one day I could live up to that standard. Maybe, when life got the hardest, you found out the most about the people you loved.

I made the walk to The Field. It felt longer than usual. I'd walked the way by myself hundreds of times, but most of the time Chuck had been by my side. We'd talk about dumb shit or funny shit, or we'd just bullshit. Sometimes we didn't even talk, because there was a comfort to being around someone you know so well that didn't require it. He was a year older than me, but we were close enough in age and looked enough alike that people sometimes thought we were twins. That was what our connection felt like. We knew stuff about the other without needing to say it aloud. And now my best friend was gone.

I turned the final corner into the parking lot and looked toward the dugouts of the baseball field. It was a very hot day and I was sweating just from the walk. If my friends were at The Field they were probably in there. All the fields were empty, as was the parking lot, but that didn't mean they weren't out of view.

Usually, I'd have heard John making a joke, followed by Marcus and Merrie laughing. Or they'd be telling him how dumb some of his jokes were. On a normal day, I'd hear them from the parking lot. They wouldn't be laughing or joking today. I crossed the grass strip and pushed open the gate of the baseball field. It rattled shut behind me.

John saw me first.

"Hey Anna," he said.

I didn't look at them; I *couldn't* look at them. The fact that he hadn't called me Anna-banana was enough to push me over the edge. Tears welled up in my eyes, and I couldn't stop them. I felt my lips pull back away from my teeth, and the crying started. I wailed, and John came around out of the dugout and caught me in his arms. He pulled me in close and hugged me tight. I didn't even have the strength to hug him back. I just stood there, arms by my side, overtaken with sadness and grief.

His shirt soaked up my tears. Marcus and Merrie came over to us and encircled me in an embrace. We stood there like that, me crying in the middle of the three of them—the remaining members of the Nightmare Club.

When the sobbing—from all of us, by the end—stopped, so did the embrace. We broke contact. I felt sadness still, but also stronger. This would be hard, but like Dad said, I would find strength and support in my friends. And we had a problem we needed to resolve.

"We have to talk," I said, my voice still shaking as I struggled to catch my breath.

I used the sleeves of my t-shirt to wipe my eyes one last time, then went into the dugout. The others went through their own rituals to compose themselves. Marcus and Merrie walked into the dugout and sat. John didn't; he kept his back to us, strolling down the third baseline. Then, when he got there, he casually kicked dirt onto home plate. I wasn't sure what to do, give him the space he might need or the speech my dad had told me. I waited, watching him cover the plate with dirt, and then he bent down to clean it off.

I went to him. "Hey," I said.

"It's my fault, Anna," he said. "I should have kept my fucking mouth shut." He kicked dirt across the plate again.

"Okay, please turn around and look at me," I said, surprising myself with the lack of sadness in my voice. I heard strength there, and confidence. John must have heard it too because he turned around.

"What is it?" John looked in my eyes for only a second and then dropped them to the dirt.

"Well, first, you've called me Anna twice today. That's not what you call me, so that needs to change. Second, we've all been talking about it the last few weeks. Who knows if it was you or me or Merrie or Marcus, or even Chuck himself?" My voice quivered when I said Chuck's name aloud, but it was out and I wasn't going to lose control again. "The only person we *should* be blaming is the one who made it happen. And it's not any of the members of the Nightmare Club."

"Yeah, but what—I think you've seen what I've seen. What the hell do we do, Anna-banana?" His mouth turned up at one corner when he said my name the right way.

"I don't know yet. But we're not going to give him what he wants. We're going to figure this out together, just like we've done everything else for the last year. We're the Nightmare Club after all, and Chuck would want us to get revenge. And that's what we're going to do." I put out my hand, and John took it.

"All right. Let's do it," he said.

We entered the dugout. John sat on the bench next to Marcus. Merrie was on his other side. I stood, leaning my back against the fencing to face them.

"Okay." I pressed my hands together. "Let's figure out everything we know. Be as careful as you can with what you say, but we are going to have to take some risks if we want to get rid of this guy."

<u>Chapter 16</u>

"It only makes sense," I started, "that we begin with Chuck's idea. If you guys like it, we can figure out how it would work. If not, we can come up with other ideas."

They all nodded. Chuck had made himself a leader of our group a few weeks earlier when he determined what we could and could not talk about with regard to Mr. Nightmare. It felt as though just over twenty-four hours after his death, I had taken the reigns from him. I was sad, and in the back of my head, I knew there were still hard days ahead—a wake, a funeral, seeing family and friends would all be hard. But my anger was foremost in my mind at that moment, and it was focused directly at Mr. Nightmare.

The police were calling it a hit and run. They were still looking for whoever could run down a teenage kid and then just drive off. I *hoped* they would find the person who did it. I wanted that with all my heart. I knew better, though. They'd never find him.

They couldn't find him because, he wasn't real—not the way other people were real. He was different. He was not human. Fear is something that lives in every single person. If there is fear inside you, you will have nightmares. And Mr. Nightmare survived based on that fact.

"Chuck's idea was pretty simple: we have a sleepover at John's house. Then, when he's there, we can ambush him or confront him or whatever. We have time to figure that part out, but we have to get him someplace where we all are. It's the only way to avoid all the secrecy. What do you think, John?"

John nodded.

"So, I don't know if he will show up or not," I said. "But if he does, and we're all there, then we'll confront him."

"Anna, maybe we should not talk so much about…you know…our friend."

"I know, I know. But I think he needs that. He needs us to not talk about him. We have to be safe and ready. If we're going to get back at him, we're going to have to talk about him. I don't think I can do it on my own."

"Yeah, you're right, Anna," Marcus said. "I'm okay with a little risk. We need to get him for Chuck. We owe it to him. I like the sleepover idea."

"Me too," John said. "But it's been forever since he's been in my room. Still, I think it's worth a shot."

We looked at Merrie.

"I'm not going to let you guys do this without me. We just have to be careful," Merrie said. "I'm in."

"We do have to be careful, and we will be. Now we just have to figure out what we do when and if he shows up."

We talked—in generalities of course—about what we could do. The whole time, we'd been unsure as to whether or not he was actually a supernatural being or just some creepy guy who followed kids into the woods. Whatever he was, he'd found a way to get in and out of John's bedroom.

Beyond all of that, there was the issue of his face. John had seen it; Merrie and I had, too. It was something we knew we didn't want to see again, an indescribable thing that terrified us all. It was both human and otherworldly. We decided, in the end, it didn't matter how many times we'd seen it; it wasn't going to change the physical reaction our bodies had to it. We were going to puke or piss ourselves, or possibly even pass out. It had happened before, and it would happen again. It was a physical thing, not a mental thing, so we needed to be ready for that.

By the end of the day, we had a plan we thought would work. We hoped it would, at least, and were ready to see it through. We had even picked a day, that coming Saturday. The weekly meeting of the Nightmare Club was being moved from the woods at the end of the Red Bird Drive to the John's bedroom. I just had to figure out how to get there. Instead of lying to my parents, I thought I'd make more progress—and feel better about what I was doing—if I just went ahead and told them the truth.

When I got home around mid-afternoon that day, I half expected to walk in the house and see Chuck sitting on the couch watching TV. I'd ask him where the hell he'd been all day, tell him that we'd been waiting for him. But Mom and Dad were sitting on the couch, and the TV was off. Mom was crying, and Dad had his arm around her. She was leaning against his chest.

"Hey, Anna," Dad greeted me with a gentle smile. But only his mouth smiled. His eyes were still heartbroken. "You look better."

Mom looked up, her eyes puffy and red, her cheeks wet. She said nothing and put her head back down against Dad.

"You were right. Seeing them did help me," I said.

"Sit for a second?" Dad nodded toward his chair. I sat in it, folding my body up by tucking my legs underneath me. I turned to face them.

"You're a member of the family, Anna, so I just want to fill you in on all of the information, so you have it," Dad said. "We think you're old enough."

Mom looked up again, wiped her eyes, nodded, and leaned back on the couch.

Dad continued. "The police called again today. They are ruling it a hit and run. No one got the plates of the car, and the only neighbor who saw the accident said it was a black car. But they don't know anything else. They will keep looking, obviously. Chuck's wake will be Wednesday, and his funeral on Thursday. We think—especially at the wake—that we will see a lot of people—friends from school and people who knew him from sports, and teachers as well as family."

I nodded. It was good they thought I was old enough to be a part of this, but I didn't want to hear any of it. I'd rather skip ahead past it all. Chuck would say that wakes and funerals were a way to say goodbye to someone who had passed away. It was how the people who loved them found closure. And for the poor dead soul to find peace, if they were religious. We weren't; didn't even go to church except for Easter and Christmas. Even that had been too much for Chuck. He didn't really believe in that stuff, but he understood it. And he didn't complain when Mom and Dad made us go. He wouldn't have wanted a funeral, but he probably would have been okay with it because it would help family and friends. Because of that—for Chuck—I went along with it.

It wasn't the time to bring up our plan for Saturday. First, I had a feeling Mom would say no. But Dad would say yes, so I needed to get him alone. Second, neither would be their selves for the next few days, probably until Thursday. I needed to wait. My parents didn't have a way to get back at the person who had done this to us, but I did. For me, the closure wouldn't come from a wake or funeral. My closure would come from confronting Mr. Nightmare, so I had to be ready.

We sat and talked for a while. Mom, who still didn't look so good, asked me about ten times how I was doing. I told her each time that seeing my friends really helped. I wanted to help her, but as hard as this was for her, it was hard for me and Dad, too. So we just had to be there for each other.

When the talk was done, I was given the assignment of finding pictures of Chuck we had stored in a bunch of shoe boxes in the basement. I thought that would be fine—hard at times but also fun to the look back at all the memories. Mom said she would help me, but she didn't want to start until tomorrow.

I didn't eat dinner that night, just grabbed a few handfuls of cheerios out of the box, ate them dry, took a shower, and went to bed. I hoped all of the commotion would help me fall asleep, but I couldn't stop thinking about ways to get back at Mr. Nightmare. I kept visualizing myself killing him, over and over and over again. I told myself I had to stop thinking about him or I'd have nightmares. The last thing I wanted was to keep feeding that fucking asshole. Eventually though, exhaustion trumped everything else, and I feel into a deep and dreamless sleep.

Chapter 17

As the days passed, I dreaded Chuck's wake and funeral more with each passing second. The image of him lying there in the middle of the street, legs and head twisted in ways that weren't possible. As much as I tried to think of something else, every time I closed my eyes, I saw that image. Not just in bed, either, but sometimes when I was just sitting around, letting my mind wander. I always ended up with the same picture.

Tuesday, Mom was starting to act more like herself. We went to the store to pick up a couple outfits for us to wear for the wake and funeral—a long black dress for each of us. Mom's had a small flower pattern on them for herself. Mine was just plain black.

I was in my room getting dressed for the wake when I overheard Mom and Dad talking.

"Charlie," Mom said. "I don't know if I can get through the next two days."

"We can. It will be hard, but we can," Dad said.

There was silence. Then I heard them move. I pictured them standing in the living room at the mirror, hugging. I needed one myself at that moment.

A moment later, there was a knock at my door.

"Ready, Anna?" Mom asked, staying outside my room and giving me privacy.

"Yeah, one sec." I was ready but stood and took a deep breath in, then exhaled. It would be hard, but I'd get through it. I knew my friends would be there. They would help me.

I'd never been to a wake before. All four of my grandparents were still alive, and the only other person I'd known who'd died was Mom's aunt. But I'd been in elementary school when that happened, and Mom didn't make us go to either the wake or the funeral. My parents told me what to expect. The wake, they said, was the chance to get to see and talk to people who wanted to come say goodbye to Chuck. They explained how there wouldn't be a chance to talk to many people at the funeral. Chuck, they told me, would have an open casket. I knew what that meant, but didn't want to think about it. I wasn't sure I could look at his face again. I knew he'd be laying there with his eyes closed, like he was sleeping, but he wouldn't be. He was gone.

We arrived at the funeral home a little after noon. There was an hour at the funeral home before they started allowing guests. When I walked in and saw the casket at the far end, I did my best to avoid getting anywhere near it. I could see only a small tuft of Chuck's dark hair sticking out the open end of the casket, and even that was too much for me.

Grandma and Grampy came soon after we got there, and Nana and Papa right behind them along with aunts and uncles and our cousins. Chuck and I were years older than our cousins, so once they came and said hello, they left. I was thankful for that.

The funeral home smelled about what I thought it would smell like. There was an overarching odor of death. And though it might have been masked by flowers and whatever else they put in the air to make us think we weren't surrounded by decaying corpses, I could still only smell the death. I would forever equate that smell with Chuck after that day.

There was a line of chairs set up against one wall with Chuck's casket set up at the end. Mom was closest to him, followed by my dad and then me. The chairs they gave us to sit in were covered in cloth, but not that comfortable. When I sat in mine, I only imagined the sadness that filled these seats over the years. No one was ever happy when they sat down in these seats, and knowing that intensified the feeling for me.

People started coming through the line shortly after that. They trickled in at first. Some I recognized from town or school. Others were friends of Mom or Dad. By four o'clock, there was a line out the door. I was shaking hands and smiling and crying with people

I barely knew. It was easy with all of that going on to forget the reason we were there.

A few friends came through, but I still hadn't seen John, Merrie, or Marcus. I knew they'd be there, probably together, so I kept my eye out. There was an hour break for dinner, but I wasn't really that hungry and the line was long. Mom and Dad asked if I needed to take a break or if I just wanted to let the people keep coming. I told them I was fine and we could keep going.

Then I saw Merrie give a half smile at me from the back of the line.

"I'm very sorry for your loss," someone said. He stood in front of me, I shook his hand and looked at him. I didn't know who he was.

"Thank you," I said.

When he walked away, I looked back at Merrie and gave her a quick wave. Behind her John and Marcus were talking. Merrie was in a nice dress I'd never seen her wear before. John and Marcus were in suits. They all cleaned up nice.

I kept saying the obligatory thank yous to people as they passed through the line, but kept my eyes on my friends. They got to Chuck and went up together. Merrie knelt in front of the casket and lowered her head in prayer. John stood behind her on one side and Marcus on the other; they each had a hand on her shoulder. Her head shook a little and her shoulders bounced even under the hands of the two boys. I could tell she was crying.

I shook a few more hands and said thank you a few more times, all while keeping an eye on my friends. They all hugged Mom and Dad and then came to me as a group. John was first.

"Never thought I'd see the day Anna-banana wore a dress," he said, and wrapped his arms around me.

I never felt as safe as when John hugged me. In less than a week, the world had become a crazy place I didn't know anymore. But when John hugged me, all the craziness disappeared for a few seconds and I felt okay. I knew he was hurting as much as I was. My sense was he felt the same way about those hugs.

"We will figure this out together, okay?" John said. "You're not going through this alone."

Marcus hugged me next, and said, "We're in this together, Anna. We got you."

I nodded with my cheek against his shoulder, knowing they did.

Merrie wiped her eyes and hugged me next. "This is hard. We love you," Merrie whispered in my ear.

"I love you guys," I said, and squeezed Merrie harder, not wanting to let her go.

I looked to my dad. "Can they stay here with us for a few minutes?"

"Sure," Dad said. "But if you want a break, you guys can go find a quiet place to sit and talk."

I liked that idea better.

"Okay, I'll be back in a little while." Then, to my friends, I said, "Come on. Let's go talk."

There was a small room I'd seen earlier. It was off the main room, and the entrance was so close to the front door to the funeral home that most people walked right by on their way in and out. So, in spite of the large crowd—the line was out the door by that time— the room was empty. There were chairs surrounding the perimeter of the room and a water dispenser at the far end with a bowl of mints sitting on top.

We were silent when we filed in. I was in front and picked a small love seat covered in the same uncomfortable floral-print fabric as every other piece of furniture. The love seat faced the door—propped open to let the long line of people in to pay their respects. I sat there because I wanted to be able to see people as they entered the funeral home. Merrie was behind me, and she took the spot next to me on the love seat. Marcus sat opposite us, and John strolled in slowly, looking around the room instead of just sitting down. He ended up at the bowl of mints, took one, and then looked to us to see if we wanted one. We all said yes, and he tossed one to each of us. Eventually, he sat down next to Marcus.

"I'm so glad you guys are here," I said. "I really needed a break."

"This is the first time I've ever been to one of these," Merrie said. "I had to ask my parents what to do before we left."

"I wouldn't know what to do either," I said.

"How are you holding up, Anna-banana? Can't be easy." John ran a hand through his hair, which I'd been noticing he did more and more lately.

"I'm all right. I haven't even been up there...to see...to see Chuck, I mean. I couldn't get close. Not yet, anyway."

Merrie exhaled. "It was hard. Harder than I thought."

"It sucks looking at all these people coming in, especially the older people." Marcus rubbed his hands together as he spoke. "They seem like they're used to coming to these things. I hope I never get to the point where coming to a place like this feels normal."

I was listening to him but looking over his head, watching people come and go.

"Same here, man," John said.

"Well, I'm glad you guys are here. I know it was just as hard to come here for you guys as it was for me, probably. Chuck would hate all these people coming to see him. But then he'd say that they were coming to be supportive of me and Mom and Dad, so he'd let them come." I smiled at the lame attempt at a joke.

All three of my friends just put their heads down and nodded.

"We're always gonna be here for you, Anna," Merrie said. "Chuck would have wanted that, and we can do whatever it is you need. Just call us, whenever, and we'll be here for you."

"I know that—" My heart sank into my gut as I looked out the door at the line of people exiting. "Merrie! Look!"

I almost reached over, grabbed her head, and forced her to look out through the door. She looked up just in time.

In front of the funeral home, looking like he'd just exited the place, was a tall man. Impossibly tall. His back was to us, so we couldn't see his face—thank God for that—but we both saw him pull on a tall top hat and descend the two steps leading out of the home. Then he turned down the sidewalk and out of our view.

"Holy shit." Merrie said.

"What? What is it?" Marcus turned around, but by the time he looked the figure was gone.

"Come on," I said, and grabbed Merrie by the arm with one hand. Then I reached back to grab Marcus, who was closer to the door.

John followed behind us.

"What is it?" I heard him say. But there wasn't time to explain.

I pushed my way through the crowd of people, some who recognized me and said "Hey, Anna" as I passed by them. I didn't say anything, just forced my way through and out to the sidewalk.

I looked down the street in the direction Mr. Nightmare had walked off in. Ahead, at the next side street, I saw the tall figure turn the corner and vanish out of sight behind a house. I didn't think he could have made it that far that fast, but I didn't want to chance it. I took off in a full sprint. Merrie, Marcus, and John were right behind me. We ran down the sidewalk as hard as we could, all of us dressed in our nicest clothes.

When we got to the side street and stopped. My chest heaved as I looked around, but there was no sign of him.

"I don't see anything," Merrie said.

I shook my head.

"What is it?" John said.

"You know who," Merrie said through deep breaths.

"Shit," John said. "We lost him?"

"Not yet." I wasn't ready to give up. "Come on."

I jogged down the side street, my friends in tow, looking in between the houses and in backyards. There was no sign of the monster that had killed my brother.

After we'd made our way down to the end of the side street with no sign of Mr. Nightmare, I slowed and finally stopped jogging.

"He's gone, Anna." Marcus put a hand on my shoulder when he caught up with me. "He's not going to just let us catch him. That's not his style."

We both stood and caught our breath. John, who had run into a few of the backyards along the way, was a few steps behind us. He stopped too. Merrie was on the other side of the street still looking between houses. I knew Marcus was right. Mr. Nightmare wasn't just going to show up at my brother's wake, let me see him, and then hang around so we could catch up to him. Not in public or in broad daylight. Mr. Nightmare was a creature of the night. A creature of secrecy and shadows. He was there to taunt us—to taunt me. If he was going to appear to us again, it would be on his terms. In his element. He would find us again, when the world was closer to dreams and nightmares and darkness.

We walked back to the funeral home in mostly silence. We were going to have to wait to confront him. There was already a plan. I just needed to be patient until the sleepover.

"If anyone asks," I said, as we approached the corner to head back to the funeral home, "I just freaked out for a minute and needed some space. Okay?"

They didn't say anything, but I trusted they knew the story.

When we made the turn, I saw a group of adults walking toward us, Dad in the lead, looking concerned. When he saw me, he jogged over.

"Sorry," I shrugged, and gave him a little half-smile.

"Are you okay? Is she okay?" he said first to me and then to my friends behind me.

I couldn't see them but knew they all nodded.

"Yeah. I'm okay. Sorry. I just freaked out for a second. I-I think it was just taking that break. I hadn't really had a break and all those people and stuff; it just caught up with me, I guess. I needed some air."

He hugged me. "Yeah, I understand that. It can be a lot. You can be done if you want. There's only about an hour left."

"No, no. I'm good. Really. The air helped. I'm fine now. Honestly. Is Mom okay?"

"Ah...yeah. Yeah, she's okay. Grandma's with her, so she's okay."

I nodded. "You can go back, Dad. I'll be right there."

He gave me a serious look that he only gave me when he wasn't sure whether to believe me or not.

"I'm fine. I'll be right in. I just want to say bye to these guys."

"Okay, Anna. I'll meet you in there." He turned and started talking to the contingent of adults that formed behind him. They were all obviously concerned about me, and I was thankful for that. "She's fine. Just overwhelmed, I think."

I turned back to the Nightmare Club, knowing I had to get back inside or people would start to worry again. "Are you guys staying or do you have a ride home?"

"My dad is coming pretty soon, I think," John said. "Then I think all our parents will come through."

"All right. I guess I have to get back in there. Thanks for coming. I have to do more of this stuff tomorrow. I know you guys will be there tomorrow too but we might not get to talk. Tomorrow starts early for me. I'll talk to you all Friday at The Field?" I hadn't meant for it to sound like a question, but I think part of me was concerned that, once we all had a chance to say goodbye to Chuck, the Nightmare Club would slowly dissolve. I didn't want that, but worried it might happen anyway.

"Of course," Marcus said.

"Yeah." Merrie stepped forward and took my hand, then smiled. That was all it took for me to know it was okay. "We've still got work to do, after all."

The four of us wrapped our arms around each other's shoulders and stood in the middle of the sidewalk for a moment. We said our goodbyes, and then I went back into the funeral home for the end of the wake.

Later that night, after everything calmed down and we were home, relaxed and feeling—I think—better about Chuck's death than we had since it happened, I asked Mom and Dad if they'd seen any really tall guys come through the line. They told me they hadn't; but it didn't surprise me. He hadn't some to see Chuck's dead body, or to see my grieving parents. He came to taunt us. To remind us he was the reason Chuck was dead.

There was a chance we were the only ones who could see him. He wasn't a real human, after all, but something else. My parents would get closure tomorrow after the funeral; hopefully. But I'd have to wait a little longer to get mine.

Chapter 18

The funeral was harder than I thought it would be. I thought maybe I was done crying after those first few days, my body drained of emotion. But the funeral brought it all back.

I finally forced myself to kneel in front of Chuck's open casket that morning before they closed it. I spent longer there than I had thought I would. Once I knelt down, looked at him and saw this face, it was exactly as I thought it would be. Chuck looked like he was sleeping, nothing more. I thought—hoped—maybe he'd just wake up, scare the shit out of me, and laugh at me for being scared. But obviously, he couldn't do any of that. He was dead.

Eventually, my parents pulled me away, and we waited in the funeral home car for them to load Chuck in the hearse behind us.

The service was beautiful—terrible. I couldn't stop crying. The music didn't help. Dad gave a eulogy. It was short and he mentioned all the things Chuck

liked to do. Mom sat next to me and squeezed my hand
the entire time. I cried even harder.

We were the last ones to leave. Then we had
family and a few close friends back at our house for
food and drinks, because I guess that's what you do for
people after a funeral. I didn't understand, but it was
what Mom and Dad wanted, so I just went with it.

John, Merrie, and Marcus were there, but with
so many family members around and the fact that I
was an emotional wreck, I didn't get to say more than
a quick hello to any of them. I was okay with that.
Today was for helping Mom and Dad deal with
Chuck's passing. I would deal with it in my own way
with the Nightmare Club that weekend.

We'd made plans to meet Friday morning at ten
at The Field, but the funeral must have drained me
more than I thought it would. I woke to the sound of
Mom knocking on my bedroom door.

"Anna, John is here," she said.

I sat up in bed and looked at my alarm clock. It
was eleven. They were probably just coming to check
on me because of…because of what had happened to
Chuck.

"I'm late. They're just checking on me. Can
you tell them I'll be right out?"

"Oh. Okay. Are you sure it's a good thing to go
out? If you want to stay home, it's fine."

The last thing Mom wanted was for me to leave
the house. Anything could happen, and she'd already

210 | M r .   N i g h t m a r e

seen the worst earlier that week. But what was I
supposed to do? Dad told me being with my friends
would probably help more than just sitting at home,
and it turned out he was right. Plus, we had tomorrow
night to prepare for, so I had to go. I still didn't have
permission, but I was acting as though my parents
were going to say yes. In my head, there was no
alternative at that point. I felt bad not being there for
Mom, but Nana and Papa were coming soon, if they
weren't already there. I had to do this for Chuck.

"I'll be fine, Mom. Thanks."

I grabbed a granola bar, which had become my
breakfast of choice this week and left without
showering or doing chores for the second time that
week. John sat on the front porch. Merrie and Marcus
stood out in the middle of the driveway.

"Sorry, guys. Yesterday drained me." I stepped
off the porch.

"It's all good, Anna-banana. We figured you
were sleeping still but got worried and wanted
someone to go check on you. We didn't want to split
up, so we all came."

We took a slow walk down to The Field.
Instead of cutting through backyards to get there as fast
as we could, we stayed on the roads, making a slow
stroll of it. We avoided passing by Marcus's house on
purpose. I realized it must have been hard for Marcus
to see that spot on the pavement every day as he left.
He could probably see Chuck lying there every time he

closed his eyes, same as I did. I wasn't ready to walk
past that spot just yet. Maybe someday I'd be ready to
walk past his house, but I'd never be able to walk past
Marcus's house without thinking of Chuck.

We ended up at The Field, but instead of going
to the dugouts, we went to the basketball courts under
the trees. There was a lone, flat basketball there. John
picked it up. Merrie sat under the tree, and Marcus
leaned against the trunk. I stood at the free throw line.
John passed me the ball, it was low on air, but not
unusable. I dribbled it and the ball bounced low in
front of me, but was still usable.

John and I played one on one for about ten
minutes. I managed to keep the score close because he
was taller than me and couldn't really move with the
ball because it wouldn't bounce up high enough for
him. Because of that, he kept shooting outside shots
and I was able to move in closer and get some higher
percentage shots off. The score was eight to seven with
John in the lead when Merrie finally said what
everyone else, myself included, was thinking.

"Are we still on for tomorrow night?"

I stopped, put the ball on my hip—which ended
the game—and walked over to where Merrie and
Marcus were watching.

We stood in silence. We hadn't talked about
Mr. Nightmare much. There was a seriousness to the
conversation that was about to happen, and we all
knew it. We'd survived earlier conversations, but each

time the topic was brought up, we knew the risk. We all knew what had happened to Chuck.

I decided I had to be the one to break the silence. "Are you guys still in?" I asked them.

"Of course," John said. The tension that filled the air around us seemed to dissipate with his response. "Especially after the other day. I'm not a big fan of getting taunted like that. And that's exactly what happened."

I caught my breath and joined Merrie, sitting with my back against the tree. The guys stood in front of us.

"I know I'm in," Marcus said. "Already got the okay from my mom and everything."

"You know I'm in," Merrie said. "Have you had a chance to talk to your parents yet?"

"No," I shook my head. "Not yet. There's just been, you know, too much going on. But it will work out better this way. My mom doesn't want me to go anywhere. She's just nervous something is going to happen to me. I kinda understand that. After what happened, she just wants to keep me where she can protect me. But my dad had this big long talk with me about seeing you guys as much as possible because he thinks it will help me mentally in the long run."

Merrie nodded. "He's probably right."

John and Marcus agreed.

"Yeah. So, I've got to get him alone and ask him. I know he'll say yes, but if he doesn't, I'll probably just sneak out like always. I need to get him alone without my mom. If I can do that, I should be all set. But either way, I'm in."

"So, that's it then." Marcus leaned his hand against the tree, pieces of bark crumbled off and fell to the ground next to me. He ripped a large piece and pulled at it. "We're really doing this."

I nodded.

"We have to be prepared for the fact that we might not get the outcome we want," Merrie said.

I shook my head at that. "I don't think so." There was a chance he wouldn't show up, or that things wouldn't go as planned, but I refused to think about it. "I think he *wants* to come visit us. If it doesn't go the way we want, we can figure something else out on the fly. But we have to get him there for anything else to happen."

The rest of the day passed without another mention of the following night. We'd already done our planning, so there wasn't anything else to talk about. There was a remarkable amount of laughter in light of the tragedy that had taken one of us that week. Chuck was still with us in our memories, and there were moments when Chuck would have chimed in with a joke or sarcastic comment. Those moments were now filled with silence instead. The empty moments were enough for us to all recognize that he was truly gone. That no one felt the need to fill that silence said everything. No one wanted to take Chuck's place. And the dynamic of our group had changed. We were still the Nightmare Club, but we were a new, different version of it. We knew it and were okay with it.

The day ended, and we all walked back together. My house was the furthest from The Field, but they all insisted on walking me home. So, we all arrived at my house and said our goodbyes. Merrie's house, they told me, would be their next stop. We agreed to meet at The Field the next morning.

When I got home, Dad said it was just going to be me and him for dinner because Mom was out with Nana and Papa. Which was fine with me because it would give me the perfect opportunity to ask about the sleepover at John's.

We sat in front of the TV for a while. My stomach rumbled, but Dad made no move to make dinner. I wondered if he'd forgotten. I figured I'd wait until the end of the show and get a bowl of cereal if he didn't say anything. But when his news show ended, he stood up and smiled at me.

"Come on." He slipped on his shoes and grabbed his car keys off the table by the door.

"Where are we going?"

"Well, we can sit around here and sulk. I could make a less than adequate dinner on the stove, or outside on the grill. Or we could just have a couple bowls of cereal. Or we could go to Gino's, get a pizza, and bring it back here. I figured you'd rather get a pizza. So, come on."

It was surprising how much Dad had changed in the few days since Chuck had died. It wasn't that he wasn't involved before; it was that he seemed to be going through the motions a lot more before—moving from one thing to the next because that's what he'd always done. Working in the yard because that was what he was supposed to do on Saturdays. Checking in with us at night. But since Chuck's death, it felt like he was doing stuff with me and checking in on me, not because he had to, but because he wanted to. It had been less than a week, and I already saw the change in him. Maybe that was the silver lining in it all.

In the car, on the way home—the pizza box warming on my lap, the smell filling the car—I decided to bring up the sleepover. I could tell the time was right.

"So, Dad…" I was nervous but just had to do it, for Chuck. "We were talking about having a sleepover tomorrow night. I was wondering if it was okay."

"Sleepover? Didn't you, kinda, stop doing those a while ago? It's fine, but is it just you and Merrie?"

I was ready for this question.

"Well, no. It's a different kind of sleepover. So, it's going to be at John's house." I kept going before Dad could object. "But it's like a kind of memorial thing. Merrie will be there and Marcus and John and me. We just— We wanted to like sit around and tell stories about Chuck. Just as a way to remember him, you know? And we wanted to do it at night and inside somewhere because, it might get emotional or whatever and that kind of thing is hard to do at The Field with people walking by and stuff. We wanted some time just for us."

It wasn't the whole truth, but it wasn't an outright lie either. We probably would tell stories about Chuck while we waited for Mr. Nightmare. I knew Chuck would approve of me stretching the truth a little. Sometimes you just had to if you wanted to do the right thing. And taking care of Mr. Nightmare was the right thing.

"I don't know, Anna. A sleepover at a boy's house…?"

"Dad, it's not a boy's house. It's *John's* house. That's like calling our house a boy's house because Chuck sleeps there." I didn't realize I was talking about Chuck in the present tense until it was out of my mouth. We were all still getting used to things.

Dad took a deep breath in.

"I— I'm sorry…" I said.

"No. No. Don't be sorry. We're still figuring all this out. We'll slip up and say things that feel normal. It's not a problem." We sat in silence for a moment as he swung the car into our neighborhood. It was nearly eight and the sun was still out, just another reason to love summer. "It's fine. I think that's really nice, and I understand it. You can go. Just, if your mom asks, let's tell her it's just you and Merrie at her house. Okay? If she finds out different, I'll take the heat. Deal?"

"Yeah," I exhaled. "Thanks, Dad. It means a lot."

The pizza tasted good, and it was a nice dinner, just the two of us. We sat in the living room and watched TV while we ate, which was something we didn't normally do. The background of the day wasn't so great, but the moments themselves were things I knew I'd remember.

When the food was gone and the shows over, I finally made it to my room. I wanted to call the others and let them know I was all set for the following night, but I didn't want to talk on the phone about this in front of Dad, just in case I slipped and said something I shouldn't by accident. I'd have to wait until I saw them in the morning at The Field. It felt as if the tide was turning in our favor.

But I was wrong.

Chapter 19

Saturday dragged. We hung out at The Field, but the tension in the air was palpable. We knew what was coming later that night, so our conversations were light and sporadic.

We left earlier than usual to rest up for the night. When I arrived, Mom and Dad were in the living room sitting and watching TV—something I'd never seen Mom do during the day. TV was her nighttime thing; she always had a million things to do during the day.

I wanted to take a nap, but as I walked through the house, I realized a lot of the normal chores weren't getting done since Chuck passed. I hadn't been in the mood to do them, and Mom and Dad probably felt the same way. Dirty dishes were piled in the sink and dirty clothes lay in a pile on the floor in the basement. Instead of taking a nap, I went around and did all of the cleaning up. Mom protested, but only once.

When I finished, I was exhausted. There was only an hour to rest before I had to be at John's house. I laid down and visualized what would happen at John's house later that night. I even visualized the part I hadn't told anyone else about—the part that was just for me. My mind was racing. I wasn't going to be able to nap.

It was time to leave so I grabbed my empty school backpack and opened it up on my bed. I threw on some comfortable clothes I could sleep in and put an extra pair of clothes in the backpack just in case.

Mom and Dad were still in the living room. Neither looked my way when I left my room, so I walked quietly to the kitchen. I opened the junk drawer and dug around the bottom for Mom's over-sized sewing shears. I'd only ever seen her use them once. They'd been buried at the bottom of the drawer for at least eight years. She probably had no idea they were there. I moved stuff around quietly and found the bright silver shears with the green rubberized handle at the very bottom of the drawer.

I opened them and ran my thumb gently against the blade, then touched the pointed tip of the massive scissors. I smiled to myself, stuffed the shears in my bag, and wrapped my clothes around them. Then I went into the bathroom. I closed the door and grabbed a few tampons from under the sink. That way if Marcus and John looked in my bag, they would immediately back away. I didn't want them finding the shears. That way I only had to worry about Merrie going through the bag.

I slung the bag on my back, said goodbye to my parents, and left. The mood was somber when I arrived at John's house. We'd already figured out where each of us would sit because we wanted to be spread out all over the room so Mr. Nightmare couldn't corner us. John had a couch in his room and a desk chair as well as his bed. We were going to be up for a while and everyone needed a spot to get comfortable. Since the bed was big enough for two people, Merrie and I would share the bed, which left the couch and the floor for John and Marcus.

Before Chuck had died, I'd had many thoughts about what it would be like to be in John's bed. The Anna from a few weeks earlier would have had butterflies in her stomach thinking about that prospect. However, I was a different person when I stepped into John's bedroom that night. The feelings were still there, but that night was not about crushes or fun with my friends. We were there to work. The others knew that too, hence our dour mood.

We made small talk for a while and eventually the discussion turned to Chuck. That made me happy because, even though he wasn't there, he was still a part of our group. Also, it meant everything I had said to my dad was the truth. I just left a few details out.

"So, I have a story about Chuck I don't know if anyone here knows," Merrie said.

I looked at her, confused. Merrie and Marcus had only really started spending time with us about a year before and I was usually with Chuck or Merrie. So I couldn't think of a time when Chuck and Merrie were there with no one else around.

Merrie smiled; it was obviously a good memory.

"If I had to bet, I'd say Chuck wouldn't even remember this. It was probably just like a small thing for him, but at the time, it was a huge help to me. We'd just moved into the neighborhood; I don't know…a few weeks before and—"

"Hold on," John said. "Sorry, Merrie. Can we make a ruling on this one? Memorial meeting of the Nightmare Club. We're all up this week. Merrie tells her story and then anyone else can share stories too, but if anyone dreams about Chuck, he gets the points."

We all smiled.

"Sounds good to me," I said, knowing they would wait for me to make a decision one way or the other.

"Quick vote," Marcus said. "Everyone is up this week."

We all put our hands up.

Merrie continued. "Awesome. I like that. I don't think Chuck ever got enough credit for how nice he was. Like I was saying, he might not remember it. Or if he did, he might not even realize that it was me. We'd just moved into the neighborhood. My dad was working crazy hours because we'd moved here for his new job and my mom was trying to unpack us, and my sister was just a toddler.

"Mom was just really stressed out. There were a lot of days where she would just send us out into the yard and tell me to keep an eye on her. I was mature enough, I guess, back then—but I didn't know what to do with a toddler for three hours while my mom unpacked. So, we ended up playing outside in the yard or the driveway. We didn't have many toys or anything because they were still packed up. We also didn't know anyone in the neighborhood who could help us out. It was us and only us, and that was a hard time for me.

"Anyway, we were outside playing—me and my sister—and Chuck walked by. I kind of ran over to him, because I'd seen him walk by before and he might have even waved at me once. When I got to him, I explained our situation and asked him if there was a playground nearby. He told me it was really close and that we could walk there.

"That day after lunch, I convinced Mom to take us there. My sister was in a stroller, and Mom and I walked down to The Field. We played at the playground all afternoon—on that metal slide, the merry-go- round, and we just ran around some, too. It doesn't sound like much fun now, but it was just what we needed then. It ended up being a really nice day, and it kind of changed the way our time here went because we had fun together instead of me trying to corral my sister in the backyard for an entire day. I never forgot Chuck's part in that and was always thankful he was there when we needed help."

"Wow," I said, feeling tears well up in my eyes but refusing to let them drip out.

I'd decided that this night was about Chuck, getting what I hoped would be some measure of revenge. But I'd also decided I needed to keep my sadness about what had happened to him locked up inside of me for the night. If I got sad or emotional, I wouldn't be able to do what I needed to be done. So I had to stave off the tears. Merrie's story made that harder, but not impossible.

"I don't know if he would have remembered that or not," I said. "He never mentioned anything like it to me."

"Yeah, me either," John said.

Marcus shook his head.

"Doesn't mean he didn't remember," I said, "but like you said, it was a long time ago and it was just a passing thing. Only a minute if that, right?"

"Yeah. I wouldn't remember it either if I hadn't made a mental note that day to find out who the boy was so I could say thank you. I guess I did and never got…never got the chance." It was Merrie's turn to tear up.

"It's okay," I said. "Listen, you told us now, and that's just as important. We're here for him tonight. He'd want us to be here, and he'd want you to tell that story. You know he didn't help you out that day so he could hear you say thank you. He helped because it was the right thing to do. We have to keep him in our heads tonight, and he'll be here with us. We are strongest with him, but can be just as strong *for* him. Okay?"

I gauged each member of the Nightmare Club by looking into their eyes. I needed to know they had their heads in the game. "We can have this night and make an attempt at revenge, but we can't let the sadness creep in. These last few days were a time for sadness, and there will be time for sadness again…when we don't need to be focused. No sadness tonight. Just focus. We need to be ready."

If you'd asked me before that night if I thought I was good at giving inspirational speeches, I would have said no. I don't know if I was any good at it after that night, either. But I saw the look in their eyes as if some part of what I'd said was resonating with them. They were ready. Part of me wanted to let them in on my little secret. It was tearing at me to tell them about the shears. But a voice in my head—I liked to think it was Chuck's voice—told me that doing so would ruin the whole thing because they'd be waiting for it if Mr. Nightmare appeared. Somehow, that would lead to Mr. Nightmare knowing it was coming. The only way it would work was if it came by total surprise. So, I kept my mouth shut and let the night unfold naturally.

The rest of the Memorial Nightmare Club meeting went as smoothly and normally as it could. After Merrie's story about Chuck and my little speech, there was a bit of awkward silence. But as usually was the case with our group of close friends, the silence didn't last. Before long, we'd all shared stories about Chuck and were talking and laughing and joking, so time passed quickly.

It was late and though we'd all prepared to stay awake for the entire night, it was proving more difficult than we had thought. I surprised myself by being the first one to drift off. I was laying on my stomach in John's bed. Merrie was in the same position next to me. I felt my eyes close a few times. At first, they felt like really long blinks, but I recognized my body telling me to get some rest.

"Hey, Anna. You doing all right over there?" Marcus had noticed my eyes closing for a little too long.

My eyes snapped open, and I shifted around so I was sitting up on the bed. "Shit. Thanks."

If this had been a normal sleepover, I would have been teased for falling asleep before anyone else. Maybe my friends would have played a joke on me, put my hand in warm water or something like that. But this wasn't a normal sleepover. We had a mission, so we came up with solutions together.

"We don't all have to stay awake, right? As long as we wake the sleeping ones up if something happens?" Merrie said.

"I just worry we might be a situation where we won't be able to wake up if things start happening," I said.

We still didn't know how strong or what kind of powers Mr. Nightmare possessed. His face was strange, and he could apparently appear from thin air, but beyond that, he was a mystery to us. So we had to be ready for anything. That meant making sure all of us were at full attention the entire night.

"Yeah, Anna," John said. "You know, you're probably right. It's better to make sure we're all fully awake, just in case." He usually had a joking smirk on his face, but even his cute half-smile was gone. This was getting serious.

"Let's get up then." Marcus stood up from his spot at John's desk. "Move around and switch positions and stuff. Get the blood flowing. I'm feeling a little tired too, to be honest."

We all followed suit. I got up off the bed, and Merrie rolled off onto the floor and then stood up. John was the last one up. He stood from the couch and stretched his back and arms. I twisted side to side. My back cracked and popped as I turned one way and then the other.

"Anna, was that your back?" John said.

I laughed. "Yeah. I can only do it like once a day. I crack it like that every morning. It feels so good afterward. But I guess laying on the bed for that long made it tighten up again."

This got us all into a competition—as always—showing off which joints we could crack. Marcus could crack his back, too. John always cracked his knuckles, and it wasn't news to any of us. Merrie had never cracked anything and, even after showing her how we did it, she couldn't.

It was a little past midnight when we sat back down.

"It's crazy because when we go out to Nightmare Club meetings on Saturday nights, we're out later than this and I'm never as tired as I am right now," Merrie said.

"Yeah, 'cause we're up and moving and stuff, not just sitting on our asses waiting for something to happen," Marcus said.

He walked across the room and grabbed a can of Coke from the pile we had brought to help us stay awake. We only had six and were trying to hold off on drinking them as long as we could, but now felt like as good a time as any. He looked at each of us, and we all nodded. He took the whole six pack and handed them out. We stood in a circle, sodas in hand, drinking and doing our best to remain in motion to keep ourselves awake.

We finished the sodas and fell into another silence. It wasn't awkward this time, just contemplative. We didn't have to talk to know we were all thinking of the same thing. The moving and the Cokes helped, though, because I wasn't feeling so tired then. And my eyes weren't drooping like they had been earlier on the bed.

Eventually, we returned to our assigned spots in the room. At first, we all stood near our individual areas, then one by one, we all returned to seated positions. There was a smattering of conversation and laughter here and there, but it wasn't constant. We were relaxed—four friends who were close spending time together. It was the most normal we'd been since Chuck had died. It was good to feel that way.

Everything was so normal, and calm, that it took us a second to realize the atmosphere in the room had changed. Something was different.

Chapter 20

"Anna-b," John whispered.

I was the closest to him, and looked over at him, then followed his gaze to the far end of his room near the window. It was the only area in the room we had left unoccupied. We'd done it for a reason, because John thought if Mr. Nightmare showed up, he'd probably come from that exact spot. When I looked to the corner, I saw a figure. It was like he was there, and also not really there—both present yet not-present. Then he began to materialize right before my eyes, out of thin air.

It was Mr. Nightmare.

My gaze remained on the dark figure, as I reached for my bag next to me. Then I glanced away from Mr. Nightmare to make eye contact with Merrie and Marcus. They both caught my eye and looked toward the far corner. That straightened them up quick. None of us were worried about falling asleep anymore. We knew what we wanted to do. I slipped my hand inside my bag and wrapped my fingers around the cold metal of the shears, ready with my backup plan.

"What do you want?" John said. We'd chosen him to speak because he was most familiar with Mr. Nightmare. It made sense to have him do the talking.

There was no response, but the shadow moved closer to the middle of the room. I could see his top hat silhouetted in the dull light of the window; the light from John's bedside lamp illuminated his shoes.

"You always talk to me when I'm alone." John's voice shuddered. "Now that it's not just me, you don't want to talk?"

Mr. Nightmare took another step forward, directly toward me.

I slid back—not out of fear, though; I was that. I just wanted to be ready. We could see more of him now. His head was down, his face—*that* face—still shrouded in shadow.

"John, you know me better than to think I'd show up here among my *friends* and not want to chat with you all." Mr. Nightmare's voice thundered around the room, but I had no doubt John's parents couldn't hear a thing. "First, I have to say I'm very sorry about young Charles. I didn't *want* that to happen, but…you knew the rules. You really should be angry at John, Anna, not me. He broke the rules, so I had to enforce the rules. There's no reason to go into details. Or maybe you're too busy daydreaming about John to—"

"Shut the fuck up!" I said.

I didn't move. Didn't stand or take any aggressive action toward him. Instead, I waited for him to get a little closer to me. That was all I needed. He might have some otherworldly power, but he was a physical thing. I could see him, so he wasn't a ghost. Once he was close enough, I was going to jam these shears into him over and over.

"Oh, maybe I touched a nerve then. Was it the comment about Charles? Or maybe it was something else I said." His face wasn't visible, but I could tell he was smiling.

"So then, like John said, what do you want?" Merrie said.

I recalled the attitude she'd adopted last time Mr. Nightmare came to visit and was glad to see it returned. It dawned on me then that Marcus was the only one of us who hadn't seen Mr. Nightmare before. Because we never talked about him in the open, the subject hadn't come up. So I afforded a quick look in his direction to make sure he was okay. I saw the fear and anguish on his face. I knew how he felt, but hoped the three of us could handle this negotiation until Marcus settled himself down.

"Always so serious, this little bitch." Mr. Nightmare turned to look at Merrie, but took another sidestep closer to me.

I gripped the shears tighter inside the bag on my lap.

"But perhaps you're right," Mr. Nightmare said. "Perhaps we do need to cut to the chase here, because I assume you're here for a reason. The five of you— I'm sorry, I mean the *four* of you…should be out in the woods right now in the little spot I prepared for you. You'd be telling your stories and conjuring up nightmares for my dinner. But you're not there. And while it might have something to do with the death of one of your members, I think it has more to do with me."

Mr. Nightmare turned in a circle, looking at each of us. He stopped on Marcus. "Now, I told Anna-banana, John, and the little bitch not to talk about me. If they'd done what they were supposed to, then the dark-skinned one should have no fucking clue who I am. But I fear that you *do* know who I am. If that's true, then someone didn't do what they were supposed to do. And *that* is why you are missing one member of your little club."

"Fuck you!" Marcus said. "Here's an idea: leave us the fuck alone. You got what you wanted. Now our friend is dead. Go find someone else to fuck with."

It wasn't exactly as we'd laid it out, but it got our basic point across.

"I don't believe we've met. I am Mr. Nightmare. And your name, boy?" The tall lanky shadow turned toward Marcus now and took a step toward him, moving away from me.

"You know who I am. Now, are you gonna leave us alone or not?"

John finally spoke up again. "We don't want to play this game anymore." He'd still had the most contact with Mr. Nightmare, but I think the anger was too real in all of us to stick to the plan. The wounds he'd opened up were too fresh. "So, let's just end this…whatever it is—game?—that you're playing with us, and we can all move on."

Mr. Nightmare threw his head back and laughed. His hat should have fallen off as he looked up at the ceiling and bellowed, but it didn't. That hat stayed stuck on his head.

I looked away in case the light found a way to hit his face.

"John, my dear boy. We are only just getting started, my friend. There is so much more I need you for. But you're right. Perhaps some of the restrictions I've placed upon you can be changed now. I'll allow you to talk about me with each other since it seems like you're going to do that anyway. I don't *want* you to get hurt; I really don't. You won't believe that, but it's true. I want you all to live long happy lives. But I *also* need to live, so I need you to continue to create those nightmares in your little group."

"Come on." I almost stood up, but managed to hold myself back. "How could two or three extra nightmares really make that much of a difference in your life? That's bullshit. You want our help? Tell us the truth."

He exploded with laughter. The four of us jumped because it came out of nowhere.

"You know…" Mr. Nightmare said, still laughing in between his words. "You know, sometimes I think the lot of you might be a little bit too smart. Maybe more trouble than you're worth. You're right, though, Anna-banana. If it were only me, well then, there would be billions of people here on Earth for me to take nightmares from. But, it's not just me. If you think I'm the only one like me, well then, you might be a little slow upstairs, if you know what I'm saying."

He tucked his chin down against his chest and began to pace the room. It wasn't a huge bedroom, but it was larger than mine, and there was enough space for him to move around.

He glanced up at John's Ryne Sandberg poster, and then around at all of us again. "But nonetheless, Anna—Anna-banana—you're right. I'm getting help from you, so I might as well tell you. It's not really going to change things in any way, shape, or form. It is what it is, and I'm here because I want to be here. I can leave when I want, and there isn't much you can do about it. It won't change what I want or what I am capable of. And we've all seen what I am capable of. But you're right, it's not just me.

"There are millions of us around. You just don't see us most of the time. You only see us when we're strong enough to make ourselves visible. And not all of us can do what I can. And I plan on keeping it that way. You just have to know where to feed to get that strong. Thanks to the lot of you—and young Charles, as well—I'm able to come and go as I please. No one can stop me, and I like it that way."

I was shocked to hear this, even though I'd seen him just materialize in John's bedroom. There was still a big part of me that assumed he was simply some creepy guy. I started to second guess my backup plan. I needed more information.

"So, what are you then?" I asked.

"Well, you *have* seen my face. You know I'm not quite… human, like you are. Mortal? Yes. But not like you. Different than you, but the same…in a way. So, here's what I will offer you. You may talk about what you've experienced here tonight and your experiences with me in general. But only with each other. I won't silence you amongst each other any longer. I won't even listen in when you're together. I fear I may have made a mistake in that. Your group has a strong bond. I just didn't realize how strong.

"But you may *not* speak of me outside your group. First, it would make the four of you look insane. They would put all four of you in a home somewhere and load you up with drugs. Drugs dull the senses and will leave you dreamless, which is no good for any of us. Second, you know too much and, like I've said, there are others. If others find out what you know, again, it would be bad for you. And for me, as well. So, it's in all our best interests for you to keep those little mouths of yours shut."

"Is there a third?" Marcus said.

"No, boy. There is not."

"What do we get out of it then?" Merrie looked up at him, she stared at his face. It was still in shadow under the brim of his hat, but watching her look up at him like that made my stomach twist. "Sounds like you need to keep eating those dreams that we conjure up so well for you. But what do we get?"

He laughed again. It shook the basement walls and the floor, as if he was surrounding us with laughter. "Such a sweet little bitch. You get the greatest gift of all." His voice changed from playful to angry in a matter of seconds. He leaned toward Merrie as he spat the words at her. "You keep giving each other those horrible nightmares and you don't join young Charles six feet under the ground. *That's* what you get out of it!"

His back was to me. He was showing emotion and possibly distracted. I wasn't a big fan of his answer either, so this might be my only chance. I gripped the shears tight in my hand, my fingers sliding against the rubber handle, point facing down so I could slam them down into his back. I pulled my feet back toward me and waited to see if he saw me.

He didn't move, still staring down at Merrie. "You should know that about me by now, if you know nothing else!"

I sprang forward, two quick steps. He turned to face me, but he didn't see me in time. Everything moved in slow motion. I kept my eyes focused on his back, hoping to jam the long shears in as deep as possible, then yank them out and do it again and again. I just adjusted my approach, took a step to the right, and I was there. I slammed my hand down as hard as I could, letting out a yell as I did.

The shears came down and pushed through his clothing and into him. But they went into him too easily, and I realized I might have made a mistake. I pulled the shears out and slammed them back down a second time. My hand followed the shears inside of Mr. Nightmare with the second strike.

My first thought when the cold wetness surrounded my hand was that I'd cut such a tremendous hole in him that my hand actually fit inside it. I waited for him to collapse, my arm feeling like it was inside a bucket of ice water. In that moment, I saw something I wasn't expecting. When my arm was absorbed by Mr. Nightmare, I could see the dreams he fed off. It was like the dreams were actually alive inside him. I saw Merrie's dream about the ghosts from Marcus's very first story. I saw my own dream about Mr. Nightmare and so many others. It was as if they were playing on a constant loop inside of him. It was only a split second, but it was enough. I didn't know if he knew I could see them or not.

As I moved my arm, I felt Merrie's dream brush up against me. The dreams were real, and I could touch them. I wondered if I could grab them. Take them.

Mr. Nightmare laughed and threw me off.

I was tossed backward like a stuffed animal. The only thing preventing me from slamming into the wall was John, who stood up and literally caught me.

Once again, Mr. Nightmare laughed.

I caught my breath.

"You okay?" John asked.

I nodded and looked at the laughing giant before me. The one with dreams living inside him. Feeding him.

"I understand," he said, still laughing. "I killed your brother, so you kill me. You get that one for free, Anna-banana. But that's the only one. And I can tell by the look on your friends' faces, they had no idea you were going to do that. One chance. That's all you get." He turned toward me.

I stepped forward, eyes down, making sure not to look up at his face, but listening for any sign that he knew what I'd seen. I didn't hear any. "What are you?"

He laughed and grabbed my face. His gloved hand squeezed my cheeks and dug into them. I struggled but couldn't get away. He squeezed harder, and it felt like my jaw would break, the insides of my mouth forced between my teeth. My mouth opened due to the pressure. He forced me to look up at him, then lowered his face, and with his free hand tipped his hat back. I saw his face, and my body convulsed at the sight of it. I puked, and the world went black.

Chapter 21

"Hey, hey, Anna-b. He's gone. You still with us?" John was next to me. My eyes were shut, but his voice was close. Someone else was rubbing my arm, probably Merrie, but I couldn't be sure. Someone else was scrubbing the floor—Marcus, I assumed.

"Fuck." I rolled onto my side but still didn't open my eyes. My head pounded; the taste of vomit lingered in my mouth. Luckily, it was mostly Coke. "Sorry about your floor."

"It's all right. He only made one of us puke. If it had been all of us, there would be a lot more cleaning to do," John said.

"I've almost got it up already, anyway," Merrie said, a bit further away.

"Yeah, we got it. Just worry about you," Marcus said. He was the one rubbing my arm.

I opened my eyes and pushed myself up on an elbow. "Jesus. Last time I said I hoped that would never happen again. Now I don't know what to think."

Thankfully, the room was dim. If it had been fully lit, I might have puked a second time. Blood pulsed through my temples and throbbed somewhere behind my nose.

"What happened after I went out?"

"Nothing much, really," John said. "He was there, holding you, and like leaning over you. Then, the next second he was just gone. He didn't slowly disappear or anything or turn into a bat or anything. He was just gone."

Merrie handed the towel she was using on the carpet to John and sidled up closer to me. I could see now that her eyes were red and puffy.

"I was worried about you," Merrie said. "I-I thought he was going to…you know. After Chuck, and then you doing that… I was just worried. Why did you do that? Why didn't you tell us?"

John walked away, presumably to bring the towel to the laundry room. He mumbled something as he left, and Marcus looked up and hurried out of the room after him.

"I'm sorry," I said once we were alone.

"I know you are. I was pretty mad at you. Like, really mad. I said I never wanted to talk to you again."

"Merrie?" I reached out to put an arm around her, but she backed away. This was serious.

"No. look at this shit we're in. It's not kid stuff. Chuck's dead. Mr. Nightmare is not human. We can't just go off on our own and do whatever the fuck we want without telling anyone. That's how people get killed. I don't want any of us to die. Doing stupid stuff like that is exactly how that happens." Tears dripped down her cheeks.

I felt terrible. "I know." I took a long breath. My head was still pounding. The last thing I wanted was to get in an argument with Merrie. But I couldn't stand letting this last even five more minutes. We needed to be stronger now more than ever. We had no choice but to talk it out immediately. "Merrie, I'm sorry."

"Well, yeah. I know you are. But I need more than that, Anna. I love you and you're my best friend, but I need to know why you put yourself—all of us— in danger like that. You know if you had told me what you wanted to do, I would have gone along with it. I would have helped you. I wanted to do it, too. But we had a plan and you just said screw the plan, and screw my friends, I'm going to do what I wanna do. I know it's been hard. We've all been through a lot, but turning your back on us doesn't help."

"No. Please, it wasn't like that. I didn't want you guys to get hurt. I-I thought… I don't know. I thought he could hear us all the time or something. I hoped our plan would work, and we'd be done with him." I broke down in tears as I spoke. "But in my head, I thought he could hear us making our plans. He knew what we were trying to do and so the only way to really surprise him was to do something we'd never

talked about before. I didn't tell you guys because I
wanted us to have something that was a real surprise,
in case he had *heard* us. I didn't want you guys to get
hurt. I wanted him to pay." I needed a hug and she
knew it, but didn't move.

"So, same as we said with John, remember? No
secrets anymore?" Merrie put her hand on mine.

The tears were coming too hard and fast for me
to talk. I'd lost my brother, and I couldn't lose my best
friend, too. It would have been too much. I nodded.

"Okay," I managed to whimper between tears
and heaving breaths.

She wrapped her arms around me, and I did the
same to her, crying into her shoulder. Before long I felt
her tears soaking through my shirt. Neither of us
moved.

We were there for a while before the boys came
back in. We'd stopped crying but the hug hadn't
stopped.

"Looks like you two are better then," Marcus
said.

I pulled back, sniffled, and looked up at him.

"Yeah, I think we're okay. Right?" I looked at
Merrie and she nodded.

"But, listen. As long as I'm not keeping secrets
from you guys, I have an idea that I need to tell you
about. Because I think we all want to get Mr.
Nightmare out of our lives, right?" I used the palms of
my hands to clear the tears out of my eyes so I could

see straight. My voice was still scratchy and shaking. John came in and stood over us.

"What is it?" Merrie said.

I sat up, crossed my legs, and leaned against Merrie. She leaned into me, too.

I looked up at the boys. "When my arm was inside him, I could—I don't know how to explain it... I could see inside him. He's not a real person. He's just cold inside. It felt like sticking your hand in snow without a glove on. Just really cold. But then, in my head, I could see inside him. I saw our dreams. I think, the way he explained it is right. He feeds off of our dreams, but not the way we think of it. I think the more dreams he has, the more powerful he becomes. But the dreams were there. Like I could reach out and touch them, grab them if I wanted to."

"What are you saying?" John said.

I looked up and my eyes met his. Merrie might have been my best friend, but I'd known John longer and our connection was different. He thought the same way I did on a lot of things. Chuck was his brother as much as he was mine, and I could tell by the expression on his face that he knew what I was about to say. He wanted to hear me say it before he would believe it.

"You guys really don't think he can hear us right now?" I said.

"I don't know," Marcus said. "But the only way we can know anything is just to go on like he can't. If things change and we find out he can hear what we're saying, then we deal with it. But we do what we can to protect ourselves. He said he'd leave us alone to talk with each other. It's only if we start talking outside our group that he's going to get involved. For now, I say we act like he doesn't know what's going on when it's just the four of us."

"Yeah," Merrie said. "And we'll do anything to protect the others."

"Yeah. Fuck him. Let's do what we're going to do." John said.

"All right," I said.

The boys joined Merrie and I on the floor. We made a small four-person circle sitting with our legs crossed just a few feet from the wet spot that had once been my vomit.

When we were situated and settled, I started again. "I think it's like he said. They—he—feeds on nightmares. But not like the way we think. He doesn't just eat them and then they are gone. I saw your nightmare, Merrie—the one from Marcus's story about the kids in the cemetery. Remember it?"

They nodded.

"I saw other ones there, too. But I remember that particular dream because it was the first one we had. I remember Merrie sitting in my living room telling me about it the next morning. They were real things. I moved my arm trying to find my way out of him and when I did, it brushed up against me. Guys, I could *feel* Merrie's dream."

"Okay, so how does that help us?" Marcus said.

"Yeah," Merrie joined him. "So, you could like, see inside him."

"No. No way, Anna-banana." John glared at me. He'd figured it out. He shook his head and held his gaze on me before looking at the others. "She wants to go back inside him or whatever and try to take the dreams out of him."

"What?"

"Just listen," I said. "Listen to my idea first and then, if you want to call it crazy and you have a better idea, we can go with a different plan. But at least hear it first. Deal?"

They all agreed, so I continued on.

"I wasn't ready for it this time. I felt your dream, Merrie. I touched it. I could have just, I don't know, grabbed it and taken it back with me."

"You know how nuts that sounds, don't you?" Marcus said.

"About as nuts as a guy running around feeding off the nightmares of a group of kids? Of course, I do. But I'm telling you, I can do it. But I won't just take one or two dreams; I'll grab them all. I'll take as many as I can back with me. He said he needs to be strong or have lots of dreams to be able to come into our world like this. So, the whole time we're having our meetings and making each other have nightmares, he's getting stronger and we're making it easier for him to torment us. Plus, he knows we meet on Saturday nights, but he probably has other people who have regular nightmares or something we don't even know about. I'll take all his dreams and then he won't be able to come here anymore and won't torment or kill us anymore."

"I don't know, Anna. There's a lot we don't know, too," Merrie said.

I explained again what I'd seen inside Mr. Nightmare, and they poked holes in my idea. But each time they did, I told them if they had a different idea, I was willing to hear it. No one presented anything different because there was nothing else we could do. John probably knew the most about Mr. Nightmare and he was at a loss. We were at a dead end. It was my idea or nothing.

With the conversation going around in circles and the sun starting to come up, we decided to sleep a little and talk about it again when our brains were better rested. Merrie and I shared John's bed. John gave Marcus the couch, and John used a sleeping bag on the floor. We were exhausted, mentally and physically. I think we were all asleep within five minutes of laying down.

None of us dreamed that night.

Chapter 22

I'd had sleepovers with a group of girls when I was
younger. My memories of the morning after were of
the smell of pancakes and bacon frying, the giggling of
the girls who woke up early, and a smile thinking
about the fun had the previous night.

That morning, the sun—which had been just
rising and changing the color of the night sky when we
finally fell asleep—was bursting through the windows
of John's basement bedroom. I blinked a few times and
rolled over in John's bed to see Merrie rubbing her
head next to me. I pushed myself up on my elbow so I
could look over her at the clock on the nightstand next
to her. It was almost noon. We'd slept late, but I knew
I was going to need to get some more to make it
through the day.

It took a few moments, but the pounding of my
head returned in earnest. I put a hand on my temples
and rubbed. A moan escaped my mouth, rubbing my
forehead never felt so good.

"Head still hurt?" Merrie's hand was still over her eyes as she lay flat on her back.

"Oh yeah. Probably the fact that I didn't drink any water after puking. Just dehydrated, I hope."

"I heard the boys whisper that they were going to go up and make breakfast for us, so I didn't really want to get out of bed yet."

"Yes. Besides the headache, I'm starving." I rolled onto my stomach and closed my eyes again, wondering if I'd be able to fall back asleep for a few minutes until the food was ready, but it wasn't to be.

"How sure are you about that plan?" Merrie's voice was flat.

She wasn't going to be able to stop thinking about it until I gave her an answer one way or the other. Also, I hoped if I could get her on my side, the boys would come around eventually. I just needed one person to join me and the argument would get easier from there.

"Nothing is for sure. But I know I could grab them. I could grab twenty of them easily, maybe more. Then I bring them back, who knows what happens? But it's worth it to me to be rid of him." When Merrie didn't say anything right away, I continued. "I don't blame you, and I won't be mad if you don't want to go along with it. I just don't know what else to do, and I feel like I have to do *something*."

"I think we should do it," she said. Then there was a long pause. She sounded like she wanted to say something more but didn't.

I started to speak a few times but wasn't sure what to say to that. Fireworks went off in my head. I only needed one and Merrie was the one I was most worried about convincing, but apparently she had convinced herself. I didn't want to seem over excited, so I stayed silent and then opened my mouth to speak for a third time.

Merrie filled the silence before I got the words out. "I hate how he calls me *little bitch* all the time. I hate when he calls you Anna-banana, too. And how he called Marcus *boy* like that? And *young Charles*. Every time he talks about one of us, I want to scratch his eyes out. I want to get back at him so he can't call us names anymore. I want to make *him* the little bitch. So, I say let's do it. Let's send that fucker back where he came from."

Merrie held out her hand, and I took it. She squeezed hard, and I felt the power and the anger rising between us.

John and Marcus came in through the door with a plate of food in each hand just in time to catch the comment about sending the fucker back where he came from. John smiled, and Marcus did as well.

"Looks like a little bit of sleep put us all on the same page." Marcus grinned and walked over to the bed, handing me a plate of food.

John handed one of the plates he was carrying to Merrie. Merrie and I sat up and slid back so the boys had room on the end of the bed. I grabbed at the crispy piece of bacon and crunched it while the others did the same.

"We were having a similar conversation upstairs while we cooked." John grabbed a second piece of bacon.

"I think we all want to get rid of him. We have to, for Chuck," Marcus said, then glanced at John. "And I don't think there's another way. We don't have another plan right now, anyway,"

I started in on my pancakes, cutting them with the side of my fork and watching the syrup drip off the piece as I brought it to my mouth.

"But there's one catch, Anna-banana," John said between chews. After he swallowed, he continued. "It's the only way I'm going to go along with this."

"What is it?" I was interested but also starving and prepped another piece of pancake.

John and Marcus shared a look before John broke the news to me. "I'm going to go in."

"What? No, you can't. That's...that's—"

"Crazy," John said. "Yeah, it is. But you want us to just let you do it. And I think you're right, it's the only way to get rid of him. But if it's not crazy for you, it's not crazy for me. I'll go in."

There was a long pause as I thought of an argument against why it should be me instead of John.

"I've seen it before, John. It was unsettling at first, then I was okay. I'll know what to expect. Who knows if you'll be able to act fast enough when you're in there?"

"You're right about that. But I'll know what to expect because you've told me every detail. And if you think of more stuff between now and when we do this, you'll tell me. Also, we want to make sure this guy can't come back here after we take his dreams or his food or whatever he thinks of it as. So, the more dreams we pull out the better, right?"

"Right?" Shit. I knew where he was going and he was right.

"So, look at your hands and look at mine. Look at your arms, I'm going to be able to grab more of those things than you just because my hands and arms are bigger. It makes more sense that it should be me. I'm bigger than Marcus, too. Of all of us, it should be me, because we have to get as many nightmares out of his body as we can. And that means the person who can grab the most in the shortest amount of time possible."

"I agree," Merrie said.

Marcus nodded.

I'd lost the argument already. I knew it, but it wouldn't stop me from fighting for what I wanted anyway. "Yeah, but….it *has* to be me."

"Why?"

"Because it just does!" How was I supposed to tell them that it had to be me because Chuck was my brother? Because when it came time for revenge, *I* wanted to be the one to get it. I didn't want John to steal the pleasure I would get when I took the dreams from Mr. Nightmare. I felt tears coming back again. "It has to be me."

"Because it was Chuck. Right?" Marcus said.

"Yes!"

"Anna-banana," John said. "When we get him, it will be all of us. We will all get him. It doesn't matter who goes in and does it. It will be you and me and Marcus and Merrie and Chuck, too. All of us will be there taking his food and weakening him and stopping him from coming here again. We'll all do it, and we'll all beat him. It will be the whole Nightmare Club—all five of us—we'll be getting nightmares, just like we always do."

I looked at them. They were right. I didn't like it and didn't want it to be this way, but they were right. We were the Nightmare Club, and together we got nightmares. We would do this together.

"All right," I said. "But I only have one request."

"What is it?" John said.

"When you get back, we all get points for those nightmares."

We smiled. The decision was made.

Chapter 23

We agreed it would be harder to get Mr. Nightmare to come back after I'd attacked him. Other than the time we saw him at our spot in the woods and the time at Chuck's wake, Mr. Nightmare always manifested in John's bedroom. Even though the Nightmare Club was important to Mr. Nightmare, we'd never seen him at a meeting, but that didn't mean he wasn't there. I think we were all aware of the fact that he might have been lurking in the unending darkness that surrounded our small fire every Saturday night. It wasn't hard to picture him there, listening to the stories with us, hearing what we said to each other, following us home, waiting for us to fall asleep, and keeping score of which stories produced nightmares right along with us.

I could see him in my head, eavesdropping in the darkness, laughing to himself when he heard a particularly scary story, knowing Merrie, Marcus or Chuck would probably have nightmares because of it. I could imagine him following us home, ready to feed off our nightmares when we dreamed. And then laughing again when the nightmares appeared before him and he absorbed them into himself once they left our bodies. I could see him spending extra time at my house after Chuck died knowing my parents and I would have dreams that were extra strong and extra powerful because our lives had turned into nightmares of their own.

In my head, he was always there, and never there. Maybe that was part of the game he played. The more you knew about him, the more you questioned him and what he could do. He was capable of killing my brother; I already knew that. But everything else he could or could not do was a question mark in my mind. When your mind starts to question everything—as it did when dealing with Mr. Nightmare—you become convinced anything is possible.

Because of all that, starting the morning after the sleepover—my paranoia kicked into another gear.

I left John's house feeling exhausted and overwhelmed, but also hopeful. We hadn't worked out details, but we knew had another plan to get rid of Mr. Nightmare.

On the walk home, I began to convince myself that Mr. Nightmare was always around. He was somehow lurking just beyond my sight no matter where I looked. If I turned fast in one direction, he was just outside of my field of vision. If I told myself there was nothing to worry about and just walked home normally, he was watching me around a corner of one of the houses, or behind a tree keeping tabs on me.

With each step, it got worse. By the time I arrived home, I expected to see Mr. Nightmare everywhere.

But I made it home, and gave Dad a quick greeting. Mom was apparently still in bed. Then I escaped to the safety of my room. I dropped my bag on the floor and got into bed. I lay there, stomach full of bacon and pancakes. I was still tired and sleep should have come easily, but my mind wouldn't let it. One moment, my brain would not stop thinking about the places I'd been over the last few weeks that Mr. Nightmare could have hidden, watching me. The next, I'd do my best to convince myself it was all in my head, that Mr. Nightmare didn't care enough about me personally to follow me around. Eventually, with my head oscillating back and forth from one extreme to the other, I fell asleep.

I had a restful, dreamless sleep, and I woke feeling refreshed and a little less paranoid than I had when I fell asleep. It was midafternoon and though we'd made plans to meet at The Field, I wasn't feeling up to it. After a quick bite to eat, I grabbed the phone off the wall in the kitchen and sat at the kitchen table to call Merrie. I told her I wasn't feeling up to going to The Field after all, and she agreed. She said she'd call Marcus and let him know we weren't going. I called John and told him the same thing, and he wasn't feeling up to it either. We were all just going to take the day and crash. We were still very much on the same wave length.

"Late night?" Mom shuffled into the kitchen behind me, her hair stuck up in different directions. She had dark circles under her eyes, and a frown had been stuck to her face for the last week.

For the first time, I noticed how skinny she'd gotten since Chuck died. It had only been a week, but it was still noticeable. "Yeah, we just stayed up talking. Telling stories about Chuck, mostly."

Mom smiled at that, but it was a sad smile, an untruthful one, and her mouth reverted back to the frown that lived there almost immediately. "That's a good thing." She sat on the chair across from me. The chair that, if Chuck had been alive, he would have sat in while we ate together. I don't know if Mom realized that or if it was lost on her. "It's good that you have a group of friends to talk to at a time like this. To talk and to…to remember and laugh."

"Yeah, they have definitely helped. But they're hurting, too." I looked down at my hands. There was more, but I didn't know if it was the kind of thing a fifteen-year-old was supposed to say to her mother or if it was something adults only said to each other. I waivered, then decided to just say what was on my mind. "What about you, though, Mom? Who are you talking to?"

"Oh…" She almost jumped back in her chair, and her eyes widened. She wasn't expecting that from me. "Well, I have your dad to talk to. Don't worry about me."

"Mom." I looked at her the way she looked at me when I was younger and told her I did my chores when she knew I hadn't. "Dad's hurting, too, right? He talks to Uncle Roy every day." Uncle Roy wasn't my dad's brother but his best friend and an unofficial member of our family. "You haven't really talked to anyone. Just a lot of sleeping. For real, I'm just worried."

The look of surprise on her face probably matched the look on my own face. Who was I to talk about these kinds of things with my mom? We'd always been close, but I was never the person to sit down and have a serious, adult conversation with her.

"Anna, you don't need to worry about me. It's my job to worry about you and…and you don't need to worry about me." A tear dripped down her face.

I shook my head. "No, Mom. Any other time, you'd be right. But right now, for however long it takes for us to get back into some sort of normal life after…you know? We're all in this together. You, me, and Dad; we need to stay strong and help each other. Dad's hurting, but I think he's all right. I'm hurting, but I have my friends and they're helping me. You're hurting, but you don't have anyone. Dad and me can't be your people for this, I don't think. Because it's hard for us, too." I wasn't sure where these words were coming from. I felt more like Chuck in that moment. But everything I said was true. "I think you need to find someone to talk to."

"You mean, like a therapist?" Mom's face looked like she sucked on a lemon.

"It doesn't have to be, no. But I don't know who you talk to about this kind of serious stuff. I think it's time you found someone. Before it's too late."

"What do you mean, 'too late?'" Again, she hit me with the untruthful smile.

"Mom, do you need me to say it?"

There was silence, and she looked at me. It was the first time she saw me as more than just her daughter. She was still my mom and I was still her child, but her eyes showed me something more than just that mother-daughter relationship. She looked at me like a friend, too. In that moment, her eyes softened and the untruthful smile became real.

She shook her head and looked down at her clothes. "You don't have to say it. I think I understand."

"I'm just trying to—"

"I know, Anna. You did." She came around the table, and I stood up. We hugged. She rested her head against my shoulder, and I realized I might actually be taller than her.

"I love you, Anna."

"I love you, too."

She sniffled and eventually went back to her room. I wondered if she would call someone or just go back to sleep. I had done what I could and just had to hope she would understand what I had said and get some help. If not, I'd talk to Dad, but not yet.

I made sure the kitchen was relatively clean and went into the living room to watch TV. I sat on the couch and flipped through the stations for a while before landing on some random kids cartoon I left on to fill the silence of the house.

After a while, Mom came out of her room, showered and looking more like herself than she had at any point in the six days.

<u>Chapter 24</u>

The next day it rained, so I didn't see my friends until Tuesday. The weather still wasn't great—clouds hung low overhead and they carried the threat of rain with them. The wind wasn't constant but when it did blow it was a cold, cutting wind that made you want to stay indoors, curl up on the couch, and watch a few movies. But we had planning to do and the need to ready ourselves for Mr. Nightmare outweighed the need to stay inside.

I donned a softball cap, took one of Chuck's sweatshirts and went to The Field early that morning after saying goodbye to a showered and rested Mom. It was a good sight to see. And I left without feeling guilty since Dad had returned to work earlier that day.

Avoiding flooded backyards, I took the long way to The Field, staying on the pavement as long as possible. I still had to dodge puddles on the roads but managed to get there with the tops of my shoes still dry. I found the others sitting on the wall at the far end

of the parking lot. In all the time we'd been going to
The Field, we'd never hung out by that wall. It was
where summer camp sometimes dropped off and
picked up. There was often a throng of little kids there
or parents waiting to bring kids home at the end of the
day. But we were nearing the end of summer. Camps
were finished for the year, and lots of parents were
taking that one last week of summer off to get away
with the kids somewhere before September.

"What are we doing over here?" I asked,
approaching the three of them.

"Grass is totally flooded." John lifted his foot.
His shoes were muddy as were the top of his socks. I
knew exactly how he felt. "But you can't see it until
you step on it."

"Ew… Well, I'm glad you went out there, so I
don't have to." I smiled.

"Anna, we have an idea." Marcus wore a
serious expression.

"Okay." I erased the smile from my face. If this
was strictly a business meeting, I could do that too.
"Let's hear it."

"Well, we know how to get him back," Merrie
said.

I looked at her, then to John as he picked up the
explanation.

"We keep having the meetings every Saturday
night like usual, but instead of telling our usual stories,
we just talk about Chuck. Or we pull names like

normal and then take turns telling stories about him. Obviously, we won't get many nightmares that way. At least I don't think we will. Eventually, ol' Nighty-night is going to get pissed at us, and he'll show up either at a Nightmare Club meeting or some other time. Then I go in and get what we need. And it's bye-bye Nighty-night."

"We hope," I said.

"You having second thoughts, Anna?" Merrie stiffened as wind blew against us. It cut through my sweatshirt and I shivered. Even though it wasn't that cold, my body was used to the summer heat and not this lousy weather.

"Not at all. Just trying to keep my own hopes in check. I want this to work so much, I'm worried about what will happen if it doesn't."

They agreed.

"Listen." Merrie crossed her arms in front of her and leaned back against the wall. "I'm freezing. Can we, I don't know, talk inside somewhere or finish this discussion some day when it's warmer?"

"What about if we do this somewhere we can have a fire to keep warm?" John rubbed his hands together, then grinned at us. We didn't need any further explanation to know where he wanted to go.

"Yeah, that will work," Merrie said. "Good with you guys?"

I nodded, so did Marcus.

"Let's go," John walked toward the end of the parking lot and we followed.

We took the street way to the end of Red Bird Lane and then ducked into the woods. Wet leaves brushed against my face and hair as I passed through them. We'd been through the woods on nights like this before, but I'd always been dressed for it. This time it was spur of the moment. Though I had a sweatshirt and jeans on, they weren't quite doing the trick. And my sneakers were soaked through to the socks.

We trudged through puddles of mud and stepped on rocks that were slicker than usual, but we made it to The Dwelling. We pulled a layer of damp sticks and leaves off the top of the barrel and exposed the dry stuff below. John produced a lighter from his pocket, which I found to be too much of a coincidence but kept my mouth shut.

Before long, the fire was going and we were warming up.

"Strange to be here when it's light out," Marcus said.

The Dwelling was silent. I could tell we were all thinking the same thing.

The remnants of the Nightmare Club huddled around the barrel. Warmth radiated off of the barrel and up into our faces. It felt nice in contrast to the cool wet air outside of our small bubble.

The silence between us stretched from a few seconds to a few minutes, I wanted to know what they were each thinking. I'm sure they wanted to know what I was, too. For a group of people who spent as much time as we had together over the year, we all seemed awkward being in each other's company today.

"So, are you hoping he comes right now, then? To get this all over with?" I looked at John, knowing if someone had a secret plan it was him. The possibility the three of them had already discussed coming here before I arrived crossed my mind.

"What do you mean?" John said.

"You had the lighter. I was just thinking maybe you hoped we'd end up here today. I've never seen you carry a lighter around. Especially the one you only use when we come here." More secrets from John. He was my best friend, but I was annoyed with him tricking us like that. I was sick of the secrets.

"Well, actually… I was hoping he'd come down here. You wanted to end it so bad the other night, I figured the sooner the better," John pulled off his baseball cap, pushed his hair back and put the hat back on.

It was the first time in long time I'd seen him do that. I was mad at him about keeping stuff from us—from me—but he always looked good when he did that. I wondered if we'd ever end up together.

"I thought we said no more secrets," Merrie said.

That comment meant John was acting on his own. Unless Marcus knew something. Either way, this was John's idea. We were best friends, yet we sure as hell kept a lot of secrets from each other. I wondered if it meant we weren't good people.

"We did. But I thought we should get this over with as soon as we could. I wasn't planning on coming here without us talking first guys. I mean it. I was just looking for a place to get warm. But if he happens to show up, there's no harm in it, right?"

"Except, there could be harm." Marcus glared at John. It was the closest thing to anger I'd ever seen on his face.

"Listen, he shows up, I'm just gonna dive at the guy, grab those dreams, and get the hell out. It will work. You ever seen me run? I'm fast like that." John danced around and took a quick lap around the fire. He'd read his crowd, so it was hard to stay mad at him.

Merrie and I laughed. Marcus tried to remain serious but smiled as well.

"So, what do we do now?" Merrie asked. "Just stand around here?"

"Well, now *little bitch…*" His voice came from everywhere. It was above us, behind the trees, and right in front of us. Mr. Nightmare was everywhere and nowhere. "I believe this is the point in time where you choose names from a hat and tell scary stories. Isn't it?"

I'd jumped, and was looking around but didn't see him. John was poised next to me, searching. I could tell he meant to get his job done quickly if he got the chance.

"You know," Merrie said in the same tone she only used when talking to Mr. Nightmare. I liked this version of her. "I hear him but I don't *see* him. He's afraid of a bunch of kids. I guess I know who the *real* little bitch is."

"Yeah, I think you're right, Merrie." Marcus laughed, and I couldn't help but laugh with him, though I was scared out of my mind.

Leaves shook in the trees around us. Not in one specific spot, but all around us at once, like a strong wind was cutting through the woods. Branches broke, just a few at first, and then more, as if a giant was stomping straight for us.

Mr. Nightmare was pissed.

"Why are you here, anyway?" I said. "I thought we had an understanding. Nightmares and you leave us alone, right?"

His laughter replaced the sounds of branches snapping.

"After the way that little bitch just treated me?" His voice came from a specific spot now, as if he had just materialized.

Merrie exhaled, but I spoke before she got the chance. We needed him closer for John to make a run at him. "Come on now. How many times have I heard you call her a bitch? You just expect her to sit there and take it? If we have an understanding, then I'm not sure why you're here at all. If we don't, then why are we planning to come here Saturday nights to tell stories? We had a deal, and the only one breaking it right now is you."

I watched the area of the woods where his voice emanated, waiting for that tall lanky form to appear and come at us. A tree fell toward us, landing with a deafening crash just outside the circle of fallen logs we usually sat on. Another one fell, this one smaller, the top of it hitting the ground at about the same distance away from us.

"What the hell?" I whispered.

"Guys, I might have forgotten to say something. Not on purpose, just a mistake. Let me fix it." John whispered back. He raised his voice to talk to Mr. Nightmare, and said, "I'm sorry. It's my fault, I think. I-I just forgot about this part of the deal, until— You know, until you just showed up here all pissed and stuff. It's my fault really. We'll leave and that can be the end of it, okay?"

"What are you talking about?" Marcus said.

John waved a hand at him, still crouched low, ready to take off the moment he saw an opening.

"I'll tell you what he's talking about." Mr. Nightmare pushed through the line of trees and stood about twenty feet from where we huddled.

<u>Chapter 25</u>

I waited for John to make his move, but he stayed where he was. Mr. Nightmare was a little too far away for John to sprint straight at him. John needed to come at him from the side or the back and have him be a lot closer.

"Great," Marcus said. "As long as someone tells us what's going on."

"Well, John, should I tell them or do you want to?"

"I wasn't supposed to bring you here during the day," John said quietly and quickly without any pauses.

"It's more than that, but he is essentially correct. The five of you—I mean the *four* of you... Sorry I keep doing that. You are not to come here during the day. When I realized you were here, I thought I should come visit. Remember, ladies, when you made your trip here back in the spring? I came to visit shortly afterward. When I realized it was the two

of you and that you had no idea you weren't supposed
to be here, I knew John had kept his fucking mouth
shut. Which is why I let you go. But John *knows* he's
not supposed to come here. He's known since the first
time we spoke. I don't think, even for a moment, that
you forgot the rules, John. Though I assume it's
possible you forgot to tell your friends. Which leaves
me with one question: why are you here?"

I never wanted to agree with Mr. Nightmare,
but he was right about one thing. John hadn't forgotten
the rules, same in regard to telling us. He'd brought us
here on purpose, to end this once and for all. I liked his
enthusiasm, but he could have let us know. I guess I
could say the same thing about my actions with the
shears.

John and I were more alike than I realized.

"Listen," John said. "We were cold. Summer's
almost over, you know? We needed a fire, and there's
not really any other place we could do that. I just... I
wasn't thinking. Please just leave us alone. This won't
happen again. I'm sorry."

"I wish I could believe you, John. But, I don't."
With the last word he spoke, Mr. Nightmare
disappeared.

I looked around, thinking maybe he was really
gone, but trees fell behind us, on the opposite side of
the circle from where Mr. Nightmare had been. Two,
three loud cracks, all coming from the same area.

He reappeared between the felled trees, his head tilted down, giving us a reprieve from that face.

John was on the wrong side of the barrel now to make a move toward our nemesis. I set us up, but understood why he'd kept it a secret. He was just trying to end this, for Chuck. And he needed our help. I put my anger to the side and decided to help. When this was over, we could deal with the fact that neither of us were very good at sharing our ideas. The only thing on my mind then, was getting revenge for Chuck.

"You made your point," I took a step to the side. Not toward Mr. Nightmare, but not away from him either. If John was going to get his chance, we needed Mr. Nightmare to look in some other direction. When we stood around all huddled together, it made it easy for him to follow us. "I get it. John fucked up. That means we get to see the tree trick? I mean, it's impressive, but what's the point? It's just a mistake. We're not supposed to be here, so just leave us alone and we will go home. No harm, no foul."

I knew what he would say, but his response didn't matter. It was just a chance to distract him and hopefully catch him off guard. He didn't like it when we stood up to him and seemed to get pleasure when we were afraid of him. So any chance to do something he didn't want us to do was helpful.

I moved a few more steps away from the barrel.

"Yeah, for real." Marcus had caught on and moved in the opposite direction from the way I was headed. "If we did something we weren't supposed to do, just explain it to us and that's it. We don't need to see the tree thing. Unless you just want to scare us or show off your magic powers or something."

"If we're not supposed to be here, we can just go home. It's fine." Merrie joined in, and I knew she would get him.

We all moved, slowly, but in different directions. John remained still, as did Mr. Nightmare. We just needed him to start moving toward one of us.

A deafening crack of wood split the silence of the forest, we all jumped and crouched low to the ground. Trees toppled around us. Seven or eight large trunks slammed down to the ground, but none of them came close to hitting us. The circle we sat in for so many meetings was surrounded by an even larger circle of fallen trees. They didn't block our escape but certainly would slow us down.

"No, no, no." Mr. Nightmare's voice echoed. "No one is leaving. You are here for a reason, because John is not stupid. Anna-banana, you're not stupid either."

Mr. Nightmare took a step toward John. We had to keep him occupied.

"Jonathan brought you here, Anna-banana, and Marcus and little bitch, because he wanted all of us here together. Didn't you John?" He walked toward the center of the circle and nodded as he stared at John. "Yes, you did. I can see it on your face."

Wind blew through our circle. It cut through my sweatshirt and chilled me. It wasn't just the late summer breeze; it was bitter cold and not of this world. The wind was part of whatever Mr. Nightmare did in the woods.

What else could he control?

"I can tell by the look on your faces that you don't know exactly what John is planning. Is it possible that you are angry with him, yes? Yes, I think it is most assuredly possible. You're angry at him because you didn't know you weren't supposed to be here. But here we are."

I circled as far away from the flaming barrel as I could without stepping over any of the trees. Branches and leaves littered the ground, so movement was more difficult. When I couldn't travel any more to my left, I stopped.

"But none of that really matters. You're here, and you get to see my tree trick." Mr. Nightmare laughed. "Because I'm not going to let you leave until I find out what it is John wanted. When I know that then I will *think* about letting the four of you leave here alive. If I don't like John's answers, more trees will fall. Maybe they will hit you, maybe they won't. That will be a bridge we cross when we get there. But weather like this can bring about storms, and that could mean an isolated tornado. It wouldn't be out of the realm of possibility if that tornado touched down out here in the middle of nowhere, would it? That would be a terrible accident. Hopefully, young Jonathan, you give me answers I like and we can all go on our way. Then maybe we can keep the deal we made in your bedroom. If not… Well, like I said, we'll just have to wait and see."

Mr. Nightmare stood facing John, focused on him more than the rest of us. I don't think it mattered what we did. He was there for John. This was our best chance to pull those dreams out of him, but John wouldn't be able to do it.

I made eye contact with Merrie first, then Marcus. They both seemed to realize the same thing. It would have to be one of us. And I think we all realized Merrie was in the best position to make a run for it.

"I don't know what else to say," John said, his back to the barrel. Mr. Nightmare was too far away for him. "It was just a mistake."

"I do not believe that. You're too smart to make a dumb mistake like that. Why are we here? Why am I here? You wanted me here, and that's why you came. Now why am I here?" Mr. Nightmare was shouting by the end.

Trees shook around us. Another crack split the atmosphere from somewhere in the woods. Another tree fell, this time right in the middle of the circle. It missed all of us, but it was clear Mr. Nightmare could drop the trees and have them land wherever he wanted.

Merrie took a few more steps, circling Mr. Nightmare until she was almost behind him. Then she took a few steps closer to him. She would get there as long as he didn't whip his head around. But what would happen if she couldn't get enough dreams to send him back where he came from?

I gave Marcus a subtle shake of my head. He transmitted my thoughts to Merrie, because she was out of my line of sight. She took another step and was back into my view, her mouth tight. Her eyes narrowed.

She was going to go for it.

"What will it be, young Jonathan? I'm waiting for an answer. Perhaps I will leave, but please give me an answer I like and do not lie to me. I will not like that very much."

Merrie's eyes widened and she took two hard, sprinting steps toward Mr. Nightmare. He didn't move, but there was a loud crack.

I looked up to see a huge branch hurtling toward the ground above Merrie's head.

"Merrie, look out!" I took two steps toward her when a second crack thundered, and another branch raced toward the earth, this time in my direction.

I saw it and dove to the ground, out of the way. Merrie wasn't so lucky. My warning had alerted her, but she hadn't gotten completely out of the way. She was on the ground, screaming and holding her leg, which was trapped under the massive branch.

I scrambled to my feet. Marcus ran to her, but Mr. Nightmare had different plans.

"No one moves or I'll drop another one right on top of the little bitch! And some on the rest of you as well. Just another accident like the one that took Charles… Right, Anna-banana?" He laughed but remained motionless, still looking straight ahead at John.

One of us needed to get to him, but I couldn't see a way out of this. He apparently had more power than we realized.

"What did you want me here for, John? Tell me now and you can go pull the branch off that little bitch. Or maybe you won't and we'll just leave her there to die. I know what my choice would be."

His long arms hung limp at his sides. Leaves swirled in the sky above him, creating a vortex that stretched as high as the tallest tree and ended a few feet above Mr. Nightmare's head. It was an ominous reminder of the power he still held, regardless of how stoic he remained.

"What do you want me to say?" John's eyes were wild, wide, and searching for a way out of this. He staggered forward a step, then another.

"Just the truth, young Jonathan. It's all I've ever wanted."

"The truth?" John slid his feet forward again, getting himself another six or eight inches closer to Mr. Nightmare. Merrie's sobs and the rustling of the leaves played a haunting backing track to John's slow progress forward. "The truth is, well… It's complicated."

"Just tell him, John. Who gives a shit?" Marcus said.

At the sound of Marcus' voice, Mr. Nightmare twitched. It was a small movement, but I saw it and wondered if Merrie had too. She was the only one in a position to get Mr. Nightmare to turn.

"Just tell him?" John slid forward another few inches.

"Just fucking tell him," I said, carrying on the fake argument.

Mr. Nightmare cocked his head to the side, allowing John to move another inch or two closer.

"See, even your friends want to hear the truth. Please, just end this for all of us."

Merrie let out an earsplitting scream, and I turned to look at her. We all did.

Including Mr. Nightmare.

Chapter 26

John sprinted toward Mr. Nightmare, but what I saw moved in slow motion, like it had been when I tried to stab him a few nights before. Mr. Nightmare had turned, presumably to glance back at Merrie and could have seen John in his peripheral. But John knew it would be his only chance and he had to take it. He didn't slip on the dead leaves or slick dirt; he was sure-footed like anyone who knew him would have expected. He was competitive and this was the ultimate challenge—life and death.

Mr. Nightmare turned back as John approached at full speed, head down, running at the man who had killed our best friend.

The wind gusted and swirled around us. The trees shook and bent first one way and then the other. I looked skyward for any branches and then back at John and Mr. Nightmare. But that glance away was enough. John wasn't there. He was gone. Inside Mr. Nightmare.

The tall man with the unreal face threw his head back and screeched. I'd never heard anything like it, so loud and long. It sounded like the screech of a hawk, but with the volume turned up and much higher pitched. I covered my ears as Mr. Nightmare writhed and twisted in obvious pain. His body faded in and out, solid in one moment and translucent the next.

Merrie and Marcus both smiled as they watched. I realized I was smiling too, but there was no sign of John.

The screeching continued, then softened, weakened. Mr. Nightmare was less solid, more translucent. His body faded one last time, then John materialized next to him, kneeling on the ground, arms across his chest like he was holding something.

My smile grew.

Mr. Nightmare, permanently translucent, rose to his feet and stood next to John, his top hat still on, face hidden. "You little fuckers!" He opened his mouth to say more, but no sound came out.

We'd finally shut him up.

He flickered in and out of existence, his body in obvious pain, first standing, then curled up in a ball on the ground surrounded by the branches and leaves that had fallen during his final stand. After a few minutes, he began to disappear for longer intervals. He'd be gone for nearly a minute at a time, blink into our field of vision once more, and then disappear again. Then, one time, he disappeared and never returned.

We watched the area where he'd been for what felt like a long time, but was probably only a minute or two. He never reappeared.

At some point during Mr. Nightmare's disappearing/reappearing act, John collapsed down on his hands and knees, his back heaving as he tried to suck in deep breaths.

Merrie let out a cheer in spite of her pain, and it broke our trance. The branch still had her pinned to the ground. Marcus ran to John, and I sprinted past him to Merrie.

"Anna!" Merrie held out a hand, and I took it, then looked down at her leg. It was trapped under the branch, but I didn't see any blood. And it didn't look broken.

"Are you okay?" I asked, breathless.

"Yeah, I made it sound worse than it was," Merrie grabbed at the branch trapping her leg. "Just couldn't get this off."

I lifted with her and the branch came up just enough for her to slide her leg out. She grimaced.

"Sure you're okay?" I looked back over my shoulder to John who was still collapsed on the ground, Marcus kneeling next to him.

"Yeah, let's go." She pushed herself to her feet, groaned again, then limped over to John. I walked next to her, took her arm and slung it around my neck.

"Marcus?" I said as we approached.

He looked up. "I don't know. He's breathing but hasn't moved or said anything yet."

We knelt next to John. No one spoke. He was curled in a semi-ball, face down on the ground, one leg curled up underneath him, the other stretched out behind him. His back rose and fell, so I knew he was breathing, but I was afraid to touch him. I think we all were.

"What do we do?" Merrie said.

"I don't know. I think we just wait," Marcus said.

Marcus put a hand on his back and rubbed.

"John." I tried to sound as soft and soothing as I could. He'd done it. Mr. Nightmare was gone, and John was still here. If Mr. Nightmare could come back and kill us all, I was sure he would have. That logic was the only thing making me think he was really gone. "John, can you hear me? You did it. You got him."

We sat for a while. I don't know exactly how long, but eventually John groaned, curled up, then pulled his legs under him and laughed.

"We did it." He looked like he was about to push himself up on his knees. His hat was still on, his face still down against the ground. "I got that son of a bitch. We really got him, didn't we?"

He sounded like himself, but there was something different about his voice. It sounded like there were three or four of him talking all at the same time at slightly different pitches.

"John, do you feel okay?" Merrie leaned toward him, like she was going to rub his back, then slid herself back instead. She must have heard the change in his voice too.

"I feel great." He laughed again.

In spite of the slight change in his voice, there was something about hearing him laugh that made me feel good. I started laughing too. Soon, Marcus and Merrie were laughing, too. It was infectious. We sat there on the wet ground in the woods, in the middle of The Dwelling, a place that had been our second home for almost a year, and laughed. We laughed until my stomach hurt.

"We got that fucking bastard," Marcus said between deep breaths.

John nodded, but still hadn't made it to his feet. Still hadn't even got up to a sitting position.

"John, do you want to sit up, or stand up?" I asked. "What was it like in there? How many did you get?"

"Anna-banana," he said—the joy and happiness audible in his voice. He talked fast, like he always did when excited, and I just let him go and tell his story. "They shrink when you grab them. He could feel me taking them and wanted me out, but there was nothing he could do. I could have stayed forever. The more I took, the more they appeared. I saw all our dreams, and so many others. They were everywhere.

"I grabbed them and was ready to leave, and they became small. You know, real small. So, I grabbed more. Like hundreds, thousands, even more. I could hold them all so easily. So, I grabbed more, because I wanted to make sure he was gone for good. You know, totally gone. I grabbed more, and more appeared, and I took those too. I don't know how many I took total, maybe a hundred thousand, maybe a million. But guys, I took them all. I kept grabbing and they kept shrinking, so I kept taking them until they stopped appearing. I had them all in my hands and then everything went dark. I-I think I killed him."

"Where did they go?" Merrie said.

"I don't know. When I left his body, they were gone. Just gone, and I felt weak and kind just collapsed."

John pushed himself up on his knees, his head still down, hat covering his face.

I felt my heart drop. "John, did you eat them?" My voice shook as I realized that was exactly what happened.

"I don't know." He pushed himself up into a sitting position. His hair hung over his face, so he took his hat off and pushed it back.

That's when I saw his face.

The world swam and spun. The trees around me bent in one direction and then the other. It wasn't

John's face—not anymore. Warm wetness soaked my crotch.

"Anna?" Merrie's voice came through the spinning world but sounded far away. I wanted to tell her not to come near me, not to look at John's face, but couldn't get the words out.

His face held me, and I tried to stay conscious, but the world spun again.

"No!" My eyes fluttered, as I looked into his face. I tried hard to hold on to the world. I didn't want it to be true. If I passed out, that would make it true. But it wasn't John's face. It wasn't a face at all.

I puked. The ground rushed closer. Black.

I woke to Merrie's voice. Marcus was there with me, too. I heard crying, but it wasn't from either of them.

On the other side of the circle, as far away from the fire barrel as he could get, John sat in tears. I was still dizzy, but forced myself to my feet. My mouth tasted horrible, so I spit two times into the dirt.

"Anna, just sit for a minute," Merrie said, trying to hold me down.

"No," I shrugged her off and took a few steps away from her.

I went to John, and sat down next to him. Merrie and Marcus came with me, all three of us making an effort to keep our distance.

"You have to stay away," he said. "You can't get too close."

"I know, but we're still together. We can fix this."

"We can't fix this, Anna-banana. This is different. It's what it took to kill him, but I guess there was still a price. I think I'm one of them now. I'm Mr. Nightmare or whatever they are. It's strange. Different. I didn't really notice it at first, but I'm craving more dreams. More nightmares. It's like a drug. I think this is what addiction feels like. I need more nightmares."

"Well, listen, if there's any good news about that, it's that we've got a group that can get them for you," Merrie said, her smile weak.

"Yeah, I guess," John said, and there was a long silence. "I can't stay around here forever. I've got to go find some nightmares. I have to go where there are people sleeping, I think, so that I can find them and take them."

John stood up but kept his head lowered, the brim of his hat covering what had once been his face.

"Just like that?" Marcus said.

"I can't go home and live my life like this. I- I'm not really human anymore, Marcus. I can't stay here. I don't know how this all works, but I'll figure it out."

Tears wet my cheeks. I couldn't talk.

"How can we see you again?" Merrie was crying too.

"Well, I know you'll be here every Saturday night." I heard his laugh, but would never be able to see his smile again. "Anna-banana, I want to give you a hug right now."

"Yeah," was the only word I could manage to get out.

"Listen. I got revenge for us. For Chuck. He didn't have to be like he was. I'm not evil now. He was because he *chose* to be that way. I think what I did was worth it. Chuck would have done the same thing for any one of us. We owed it to him."

"Yeah." I still couldn't say anything else. In the span of a week, I'd lost Chuck and now I was about to lose John. I couldn't take much more.

"It's not goodbye. It's just gonna change things. I'll see you every Saturday night. And maybe I'll figure out how to make the trees fall and stuff too. We could make some kick ass dams or something. Merrie, Marcus, could we have a minute." He still kept his face hidden when he spoke to them.

I moved closer to him. As close as I could get without touching him. I thought about reaching into him. I could reach in and grab some dreams—not enough to kill John, but enough to join him. If I could do that then we'd be able to stay together. My hand moved toward him because I wanted that.

"No," he said. "I know what you're thinking, but you can't. You can't do it to Merrie and Marcus,

287 | M r .   N i g h t m a r e

and you can't do it to you parents. How would your mom take it if you just disappeared right now?"

"I know, but I want to. I-I…" I couldn't get more words out. I cried instead.

"Listen, I know you like me, Anna-banana. It's not that hard to figure out. I might be oblivious, but not that much. I never said anything because I wanted to talk to Chuck and make sure he was okay with it. I just never got the chance."

"You did?"

"I knew, yeah. But you were like a sister to me. It's just a hard thing, and I totally understand it. I don't know what would have happened. But things have changed. We have to do this for everyone else, okay?"

I nodded. "I get you. My mom isn't doing too well. She'd fall apart."

"Yeah, you know they are like second parents to me. Can't let bad stuff happen to them. It's already going to be hard enough that I'm gone too after Chuck."

"Well, then we can't drag this out." I sniffled and tears streaked down my face. I didn't care how I looked so I didn't try to wipe them off or brush them away. "Let's figure out a story, and you can go."

We called Marcus and Merrie over and huddled together for the last time, and the Nightmare Club came up with a story. We'd tell the police and our parents that we'd gone to the fields and the weather was bad, but we tried to play anyway. Merrie slipped and fell and hurt her leg, and so we decided to go home. Marcus and I walked Merrie home because she was limping, and John left to go on his own. We didn't think anyone would question us as long as our stories matched.

John stood at the middle of the circle, his back to the barrel, the fire in it long since burned out. The wind blew, and I looked skyward. It was different than the wind Mr. Nightmare had created. There was no threat anymore. John had taken care of that for us. And now it was our job to take care of things for him.

"If you can, try to keep the club going," he said as he stood before us, still hiding his non-face. "Maybe get a few more members. It'll keep me going. Even if I can't visit that much, I know I'm going to need more nightmares. I can already feel how strong the urge is to have more. I'll figure this out, and I'll visit. See you guys Saturday?"

"Absolutely," Marcus said.

Merrie nodded.

"Of course," I said.

"Great." His shoulders raised and lowered once, twice, then again, but he'd disappeared before they could drop again.

The three of us embraced and cried together. We needed to get back, so we made our way out of the woods not long after.

We didn't talk, just walked out over the trees that had fallen. We had to help Merrie over a few of the trunks because of her leg, but we made it.

It had been a little over a year since I walked into the woods with John and Chuck for the first unofficial meeting of the Nightmare Club. It had been just the three of us then. Walking out, there were still only three of us, but I was the only one who had been there for that first meeting. It was a comfort knowing the Nightmare Club would live on.

Chapter 27

For a few weeks, John's disappearance was big news across the region. But, in the end, after the death of his best friend, most people assumed he ran away because of the grief or that he'd taken his own life. Even the police believed it. We did our best to convince them he would never do something like that, because we couldn't stand him being remembered that way. No one believed us. So, despite our best efforts, most people thought John was a suicide victim and that he'd ended up at the bottom of a nearby lake.

John's visits became less frequent as time went on, and his personality started to change. For a while, it was just Marcus, Merrie, and I at the Nightmare Club meetings when John came around. He'd participate, and we even pulled his name a few times, then he'd tell a story. One was actually pretty scary, and he earned quite a few points from it. But, like I said, over time he changed. I don't know if it was the way he lived, which he always told us he couldn't quite explain. Or maybe it was the fact he fed off of so many nightmares. But I started to understand why Mr. Nightmare ended up the way he was. If John could change that much in only a few months, what would years, or even decades, do to someone like Mr. Nightmare?

Eventually, at John's continued requests, we added three more members to the Nightmare Club. Merrie took on a mentoring role while I maintained my role as score keeper. When a new member was added, we returned the scores to zero.

I got a new notebook which I still kept under my bed. I kept the old one too, because the original Nightmare Club was still the best version. I took pride being in first place for an entire year in the second version of the Nightmare Club. After which, we decided to return all scores to zero and start again.

I saw the stories I told as more than just stories; they were a way to help the first boy I ever really loved. I didn't know if I'd ever love someone again after John, and I would do anything for him. So I worked my ass off coming up with the scariest stories I could think of week in and week out. Every time someone reported a nightmare from one of my stories, I thought of John.

We got older. Marcus graduated high school, left for college, and the Nightmare Club shrunk. It shrunk again and then died when I left. I stayed in touch with Marcus and Merrie throughout college and, whenever we were all in town, we'd meet up and discuss the fun times we'd had. But there was nothing quite like that first year of the Nightmare Club.

My life moved on, and apparently so had John's. He made an occasional appearance from out of nowhere, but when he talked, he sounded angry. Not at me, but at everything else, it seemed. Life was hard for him, but he never went into details about what that meant.

I created a second version of the Nightmare Club with some of the other English majors in college and it went pretty well. Instead of telling stories, we wrote them. We used the same rules as the original Nightmare Club: if you had a dream about one of the stories that was passed around, you had to let me know so I could keep track of who created the most nightmares. I felt it was the least I could do for John. Like with the second version of the Nightmare Club, I found myself winning at the end of every semester.

I just couldn't help it. I was too competitive, and I'd been through so much in my life I could draw on for stories. At times, I'd take parts of true things and twist them to make the story seem scarier. Kind of like when we first started the Nightmare Club. It was easy, and it wasn't like I was just completely making the stories up.

I used real characters, real people, and the way I described them was how they looked in real life. I just embellished a little bit here and there. I had to. I wanted to win. In the end, whether it was for John or for the competition, it didn't matter.

The most important things were the nightmares.

THE

END

Or is it...?

Joe Scipione is the author of Zoo: Eight Tales of
Animal Horror, Decay and Perhaps She Will Die. He
lives in the suburbs of Chicago with his wife and two
kids. He is a member of the Horror Writer's
Association and a Senior Contributor and horror book
reviewer at Horrorbound.net. When he's not reading or
writing you can usually find him cheering on one of
the Boston sports teams or walking around the lakes
near his home. Find him on twitter: @joescipione0 or
at www.joescipione.com